Beneath the Linden

A Novel
Based on a True Story

John Herbert Emerson

Library of Congress Control Number: 2011916648
ISBN: Hardcover   978-1-4653-6754-9
                 Softcover   978-1-4653-6753-2
                 Ebook   978-1-4653-6755-6

This book was printed in the United States of America.

Television Tower Berlin Photo on the cover by Roberto Velazco Davalos
(LouZifer ART ' N ' PHOTOGRPHY, Berlin)

To order additional copies of this book, contact:
Xlibris Corporation
1-888-795-4274
www.Xlibris.com
Orders@Xlibris.com
72748

Beneath the Linden

With gratitude to and in honor of
those represented as

Marlo, Karl, Greta, Rainer, and Margaret
Kurt, Eva, Albert, Anita,
and Hans

"Unter dem Lindenbaum!
Der hat seine Blüthen über mich geschneit."

(Under the linden tree
Where blossoms fall gently down and covered me.)
        from Gustav Mahler's
        "Lieder eines Fahren den Gesellen"
        ("Songs of a Wayfarer")

CHAPTER 1

The German Democratic Republic (East Germany), 1967

Karl Mann was relieved that the compulsory summer student military exercises were over. He wasn't lazy. He simply detested them with every fiber of his being. Karl was eager to go home and spend the waning days of summer with his family in Meissen, helping his parents, Eva and Kurt, and younger brother, Albert, with chores at the family store. Family members were pleased that Karl, with his six-feet-two muscular frame, accepted the task of lugging cartons of commodities from the basement storeroom to the store shelves.

It was a busy corner grocery on Nossenerstrasse, an upscale neighborhood in that quaint seven-hundred-year-old city. The Mann's home was a spacious apartment above the store. Karl was enchanted with his hometown, its ancient history, the world-renowned porcelain factory, and the Elbe River that meandered through the valley. *It's good to be home*, Karl thought.

On this Monday morning in late August, the Mann family prepared to open the store. Kurt turned to Karl. "Son, go downstairs to the cooler and bring up the crates of produce."

When Karl opened the cooler door, he was happily surprised by what he saw. "Father!" he shouted up the staircase. "You really scored on this supply of grapefruit and oranges!" Few markets anywhere around sold such robust citrus. In fact, these scarce commodities seldom found a place on the Mann family table.

Kurt lumbered down the stairs. "Ah, we were lucky to get these crates brought in from West Germany. You know Ernst Hofmeister, my old army comrade."

Karl nodded.

"Since January, on his business trips to the western sector, he has picked up bargains on fruits that we can't get anywhere else. He smuggles them in and is never searched. The border guards know him so well. That's how we got those oranges and grapefruit. The locals know we are able to get them from time to time." Kurt developed a broad smile, very pleased with himself. He ran his hand through his thick crop of blond hair, which showed no signs of graying. "They sell out very quickly," he added.

"I see," Karl replied thoughtfully. He bore the heavy crates up to the main floor and placed the precious cargo in produce bins near the store window. Karl pressed an orange to his cheeks and felt the coolness and inhaled the aroma. He squeezed the grapefruit, noticing their softness. What a rare treat! The fruit would surely fetch a premium price.

Karl was well aware of scarcities in the German Democratic Republic. A medical student, he was learning that certain prescription medicines were hard to come by, especially antibiotics. Communist East Germany was at the mercy of the Soviet Union for rationed drugs. The government's threat of harsh treatment of citizens caught with contraband discouraged a black market. Indeed, fresh produce, medicines, detergents, and cosmetics were in short supply. Crumbling buildings, postwar rubble strewn haphazardly, and deteriorating infrastructure revealed a vanishing labor force and poor economy. It was as if World War II had ended only weeks earlier!

To keep his learning curve at its peak, Karl visited the large city public library in nearby Dresden as often as possible during summer breaks to read current articles in medical journals. Western professional journals were rarely available except for publications from some European countries like Switzerland and Italy. Most accessible were journals from the Soviet Union, Baltic States, and of course, the German Democratic Republic. Comfortable keeping his own company, Karl became totally absorbed in his reading. Occasionally he made time for former schoolmates and neighbor friends. But books and science laboratories were his best friends. Karl had an excellent mind and applied himself tirelessly to academics. That spring, he had completed his first year of medical school tenth from the top of his class and was eager for the fall semester to get under way. He was absolutely focused on his goal to become the best physician he could possibly be. God knows doctors were in great demand!

Finally, October arrived and, with it, the beginning of classes at Humboldt University in East Berlin. Karl packed his books and a few laundered clothes and boarded the train for Berlin.

One afternoon, he stopped by the student social center on his way to the dorm. He was scanning announcements posted on the message board when a classmate and trusted friend, Fritz Schimmel, approached.

"Guten morgen, Karl!"

"Ah, Fritz. Morgen! How was your summer?"

"Good! Traveled some. And yours?"

"The usual. Helped my family at the store, did some research at the library."

"Say, Karl, I learned yesterday that some of our friends have arranged a visit with American students on Friday, November third. They're in an overseas German studies program in West Berlin. They want to talk with us about . . ." Fritz looked around the room and lowered his voice. "About . . . political economy and life in the GDR."

Karl cocked his head to one side and shrugged his shoulders. "*Political economy!* That's such a . . . a . . . a—"

"A sensitive issue? Yes, I know. But these international discussions are usually enlightening. What do you think, Karl? Want to be included? The meeting will be at one of our usual places."

Karl, Fritz, and their trusted student friends planned these rendezvous from time to time. They met at different public venues to avoid detection by East German secret police.

"Hmm. That's a week from now. Maybe." Karl took a deep breath and exhaled. "Sometimes these meetings with students from the West are depressing, you know what I mean?"

Fritz nodded. "Well, look at it this way. It's better than no dialogue at all with the other side of the world."

Karl gave a halfhearted acknowledgment. "You're going?"

"Wouldn't miss it. By the way, I understand a few of them are women. Now, you wouldn't want to miss out on meeting some American girls, would you?" Fritz laughed and slapped Karl on the back.

Raising his eyebrows, Karl broke a faint smile. "We'll see."

"Look, Karl, I'll give you a call next Friday. Tschau!"

"Auf Wiedersehen!"

By Friday, November 3, Karl had forgotten about the meeting. He was stretched out on the bed in his dorm. It was four thirty when he was aroused from his nap by a knock on the door.

"Ugh . . . mm . . . Yes?" murmured Karl.

"It's me, Fritz!"

"Oh! Come in."

Karl sat up and swung his legs over the side of the bed, rubbing his face vigorously and matting down his shock of blond hair. Then he remembered.

"I'm on my way down to the café for the meeting. Are you coming?"

Karl sat there in a daze for a moment, considering his options.

"I don't know, Fritz. I'm feeling tired . . . My stomach seems a little unsettled. I don't think I'd be good company tonight."

"Aw, come on. It'll do you good to get some fresh air and get your mind off your bellyache."

Karl thought for a moment. "I suppose you're right. Give me a minute to freshen up and change my clothes."

Fritz and Karl walked along the avenue lined on both sides with *Tilia cordata*, a European species of linden trees that shimmered in the brisk autumn wind. The tiny heart-shaped leaves whipped into the air and danced in the breeze as if loathe to touch the ground.

Karl and Fritz approached the Hotel Unter den Linden and entered the Lindenkorso Café, where three student friends were waiting. They gathered at an oversized oval table in the corner of the spacious restaurant, anticipating an unknown number of visitors from the United States. Any Friday afternoon at the Lindenkorso was wild. The place was rocking with the cacophony of youthful voices, each contending to be heard above all others. It was not the best venue for serious East-West conversation, but it was safe. East German secret-service plants posing as students would have quite a challenge eavesdropping. Even so, Karl and the others knew they had to be vigilant. The five ordered a round of beer as they waited for their guests. Soon a single male student from the United States named Ken appeared and joined the group.

"I thought there were going to be some girls from the USA," asserted Fritz.

"A few will join us any time," he said in fairly fluent German. "Since they weren't quite ready, I thought I'd better come along so you wouldn't think we had forgotten."

Fritz, Karl, and the others smiled with anticipation.

Studying Ken, Fritz asked, "Didn't I see you in one of our classes recently?"

"That's right. I was permitted to audit your political science class for a day."

"Hmm, what did you think of it?" queried Karl.

"It was different, but interesting. I noticed that students did not raise questions or make comments on the lecture."

Karl, Fritz, and the other German students glanced at one another, shrugging their shoulders.

"That is the style of lectures on politics here," Fritz explained.

"In the United States, it's different. No professor is safe from being bombarded with probing questions."

"Did you try to ask questions?" Karl asked.

"Oh, no! I was cautioned by our West German host that I was to be a silent observer. I wasn't even allowed to take notes."

"Did you say you are from San Francisco?" Karl asked.

"That's right. You know something about San Francisco?"

"Yes, I saw a photograph and an article in an encyclopedia once. There was the ocean, the bridge, a trolley car."

Karl found San Francisco enchanting from the little he had read about in the encyclopedia. He especially liked the ocean but had little opportunity ever to go to the seashore—once on the Baltic coast and once in Romania at the Black Sea. He thought how wonderful it would be to go to America someday and visit San Francisco. *That's a far-fetched notion, a vain hope*, Karl thought.

Ken pulled a small package out of his coat pocket and spread the contents on the table.

"These are picture postcards of San Francisco," he said. "I brought some to give to each of you."

There was a chorus of "Thank you!" Karl was touched by the friendly gesture.

"That is the . . . Golden . . . Gate . . . Bridge," Ken pointed out thoughtfully, helping with the English pronunciation. "It has a layer of fog across the top of the spans. That's a pretty typical scene of the bridge."

"And here is a picture of one of those little trolleys," said Karl.

"We call them cable cars."

"Now *that* is an interesting street!" exclaimed Fritz.

"That's Lombard Street, famous for its flowers and windy narrow thoroughfare on that steep slope of a hill."

The German students were really enjoying their gifts of picture postcards. Before long, they were deeply engrossed in a serious conversation about national politics, economics, and international relations. They were cautious and kept their voices low yet audible enough to be heard.

Every few minutes, Fritz glanced toward the entrance, watching for the American women to emerge. Karl, whose curiosity was now piqued, intermittently looked there too. Besides, Karl was getting restless. The issues under discussion were a repeat of conversations with other students from the West on previous occasions. It only served to make him long for that which he couldn't have.

Having female students from the West would be a novelty to savor, thought Karl, *a wonderful distraction indeed.* His attention drifted away from the discussion as he kept looking at the door.

CHAPTER 2

The West Berlin YMCA hostel was home for a number of European and American students participating in the Experiment in International Living. Marlo Farrell, her college classmate Emily McKay, and four others from the States dashed out of the youth hostel. Marlo, Emily, Judy, Kathy, Molly, and Maddy were running late for their meeting with some East German university students at the Lindenkorso Cafe. The girls ran down the stairs at the Nollendorfplatz subway to catch the U-Bahn for the Friedrichstrasse Station on the East Berlin side of the city divide.

It was nearly five thirty when they arrived at the East German U-Bahn station. They were detained for about thirty minutes, filling out tourist visa forms, declaring currency, and having personal belongings searched—a customary border-crossing ritual that foreigners had to endure when entering the GDR.

Marlo gasped, raising her hand to her mouth as if to muffle her words. "Look at that!"

Her friends followed her pointing finger in the direction of East German border guards. "*My god!*" they intoned in unison under their breath.

They gawked at a stationary vehicle at the custom control building nearby. They had never seen anything like it. One guard passed a mirror attached to the end of a pole along the underside of the car. Another guard was dismantling interior door and trunk panels. The vehicle parts were on the ground. A third guard stood erect in front of the car with his machine gun poised toward the BMW sedan. They carried out their duties with an air of insolence. The passengers of the car waited inside the control station under the watchful eye of the shift commander. Several other vehicles in line waited their turn to pass through Checkpoint Charlie. They would have a long wait.

"Do you think they do that to *every car*?" Emily wondered aloud. The others shrugged.

Maddy stopped to reach for her camera. Marlo quickly frowned and wagged her hand to signal disapproval. "Madeline! You could get in serious trouble doing that," whispered Marlo. Maddy slowly dropped her camera back into her coat pocket with a look of resignation. As they all proceeded through the confining fenced corridor for pedestrians, a guard called out to the students. They froze in place, looking back. The guard motioned to Marlo to return to the custom control station and waved the others to go on.

"It's okay," she said to the others. "Go ahead. I'll catch up."

The girls were hesitant to leave without Marlo. Screwing up courage and feigning calmness, she assured them she'd be all right. "And besides, it would be far better not to aggravate the officers," she told them.

All but Marlo finally got to the restaurant. They stood inside the entrance, transfixed in the midst of the rowdy student crowd, looking for Ken, their escort. The expansive heavy-beamed hall of dark wood smelled of aged oak, brew, and smoke.

Ken waved to the girls, calling out to them. All the fellows stood and arranged chairs for the ladies. While Ken and Maddy paired off, each of the German students offered a seat to the Americans. When the process neared completion, it appeared that Emily remained to be hosted by either Fritz or Karl. Ken instantly became the congenial referee and tossed a coin. Karl became the odd man out. Emily explained that another student had been detained at Checkpoint Charlie and would show up soon. *I sure hope so!* was her silent thought, trying to mask her jitters.

As the students exchanged pleasantries, Karl periodically glanced toward the entrance. He studied the others at the table engaged in intense conversation, noticing how well the Americans spoke German.

Twenty minutes had passed when Karl looked again at the café entrance door. At that moment, Maddy squealed, "Look! There's Marlo." Karl stood up, fixing his gaze upon this stranger with a striking pose at the door. His eyes danced across her countenance and statuesque figure. There was a sweetness in her face that he immediately found delicious. Detecting his self-consciousness, Karl became surprised and even amused by his own reaction. It was an awkward moment that seemed to linger indefinitely.

CHAPTER 3

Marlo was an attractive tall brunette with curls that bobbed like springs on her shoulders in cadence with her gait. By nature she was friendly, although reserved. Marlo was spending a semester abroad as a German major at the University of the Pacific in Stockton, California. An overseas course being offered on German music history interested her. She nearly pursued a musical career, having studied piano and voice from childhood. Marlo, like her father and sisters, was gifted with a beautiful singing voice. She was impressed with the musical stylings of Dave Brubeck, a University of Pacific grad. But Marlo had her heart set on German literature, culture, and history. Music became her minor. The university had an exceptional music conservatory.

Born in San Jose, California, not many years after the end of World War II, Marlo was the fourth of five daughters in the household of The Reverend Dr. J. Wesley Farrell and his wife, Esther. Dr. Farrell was a prominent minister in the expansive Santa Clara Valley, known for his sensitive pastoral care, his commitment to liberal theology, and his passion for social justice and world peace. His undergraduate studies had been in religion at the then College of the Pacific, later having earned his degree in theology at Boston University School of Theology—known in the 1930s as the school of the prophets. Esther had studied at San Jose State College with an interest in kindergarten teaching, which she never pursued after college.

All through elementary and high school, Marlo took her studies seriously. She was a straight A student, but it didn't come easy. She was crushed when a junior high physical education teacher gave her a B. That was the only B she ever received.

She had screwed up her courage to confront Mrs. Gordoy. "Why did I only get a B?" she protested.

Ruth Gordoy only looked into the anxious eyes of her student, gave a patronizing smile, clicked her tongue several times, slowly shook her head, and walked away. Marlo was left standing in the hallway, staring tearfully at her shoes.

To be sure, Marlo certainly was not a gifted athlete. Being uncoordinated would be a magnanimous way, at best, to state the case.

As a child, she knew how to have fun with her friends. The family's home at Fifteenth and San Antonio Streets in San Jose was a spacious two-story dwelling. She and her friend Jane delighted in plunging down the laundry shoot from the second floor. They would scarf down huge bowls of ice cream while watching *Captain Kangaroo*, *Howdy Doody*, or puppeteer Shari Lewis on TV, but especially Dick Clark's *American Bandstand*. Marlo liked to stage what she called Marlo's Dance Show, choreographing routines to entertain Jane and other neighborhood friends.

Unlike her sisters—Doreen, Janice, Linda, and Diane—Marlo had little interest in boys. She never dated. Once, she went to a movie with a school friend, Glenn. It was not a happy experience.

"He wanted to hold my hand during the movie," she had confided to her younger sister, Diane, "but yuck, his hands were sweaty!"

If, as surmised by her sisters, Marlo ever kissed a boy, it may have happened, but only once.

Marlo could be quirky. Her longtime childhood friend, Jane, planned a surprise twelfth birthday party at her home. It was a total surprise. Marlo showed up wearing curlers in her hair—a memorable highlight of hilarity for her friends in spite of Marlo's embarrassment!

Marlo's childhood idiosyncrasies extended to the meal table. She detested peas, which appeared much too often on her dinner plate. No one in the family questioned her need to be excused from the table to go to the toilet. But Janice, her older sister with a keen eye, on one such evening spotted a neat little pile of peas stashed behind the claw-foot of the bathtub—a trick Marlo learned from Linda, who also despised peas. Janice knew about that too. That escapade remained their little secret.

When Marlo was to enter high school, Dr. Farrell was appointed to serve as senior pastor of a prestigious large church in Bakersfield, California.

Mr. Lora became Marlo's favorite high school teacher at Bakersfield High, directing the music and drama department. In a school of three thousand students, Mr. Lora selected Marlo to be one of the few singers in the distinguished madrigal chorus. She blossomed because of Lora's approval and encouragement.

Parading before a full-length bedroom mirror, she said of the madrigal girls' uniform, "I'm going to wear this floor-length purple velvet dress and white blouse even to the senior ball!"

In Marlo's senior year in high school, she auditioned for the spring musical *The Music Man*. She would be perfect in the role of Marian, the librarian. She expected that Mr. Lora wanted her for that part. A freshman girl, walking in out of nowhere, was given the role. Though her heart was broken, Marlo accepted a part in the chorus in which she had a single solo line in the song about the Wells Fargo wagon—the line "And a double boiler." Typically, she always tried to please people she cared about and do her very best.

At the cast party, the freshman protégée quickly disappeared, overcome by a case of nerves. The other cast members gathered around the piano. "Marlo!" they shouted. "You sing the solos." And they performed songs from the show for each other. Her friends knew she had been shafted and deserved to be Marian, the librarian. It was a euphoric boost to her morale.

A few years later, Diane, an aspiring high school thespian, was excited about being picked for the female lead in *A Man for All Seasons*. She dashed home and ran into the kitchen to find Marlo rinsing off dishes in the sink.

"Sis!" she exclaimed. "I'm going to have a leading role in the school's senior play."

Marlo gave her a hug. Then she broke into tears and ran upstairs to the bedroom.

When she won a full scholarship to the University of the Pacific, her parents were proud. Her father was especially aglow since he had done his undergraduate studies there. Expecting she would pursue a musical career, Marlo's parents were surprised when she chose German as her major.

"Marlo, why not music?" her mother asked. "After all, we invested in your piano and voice lessons."

Marlo felt as though she was going to be a disappointment to her parents. "I can take music as a minor. I just don't think I want to teach music."

"Why German?" her father asked.

"Well, Dad, you know the community forums you used to put on about international relations . . ."

"Yes."

"I got interested in postwar European recovery. That led me to an interest in German history and culture. I think I'd like to teach that."

Her father, breaking into a broad smile, nodded approval. Marlo was relieved. Esther rolled her eyes but decided not to say anything further.

Marlo enrolled at UOP's Raymond College and proved to be a model academician. She excelled in German language and related studies. At the music conservatory, she studied voice and dabbled in piano. When the opportunity came to take a semester in Germany, Marlo was elated. She and a classmate, Emily, signed up and were accepted. An unanticipated adventure was about to unfold.

CHAPTER 4

Fritz nudged Karl, cocking his head in the direction of the café entrance. For a minute, Karl couldn't move. His feet felt like they were encased in lead shoes glued to the floor. Fritz gave a gentle shove that sent Karl off balance enough to move. He took a deep breath, composed himself, strode to the door, and introduced himself to Marlo. With a nervous giggle, she smiled and stretched out her arm for a handshake. He gave her a firm grip and escorted her to the table where the others were assembled. They all shared personal backgrounds, courses of study, and the contrast of American and East German academia.

"Say, if you have some free time this evening, we can show you some of the sights in East Berlin," Fritz proposed eagerly.

Eye contact between Emily and Marlo brought lifted eyebrows and smiles. They nodded. Karl was agreeable. He could not take his eyes off Marlo. Her smooth complexion, large hazel eyes, dainty nose, shiny hair, and contagious smile were appealing. He was impressed with her intelligence and command of the German language. There was certainly something special about her. But Marlo was oblivious to Karl's rapt attention.

Marlo's facial expression suddenly changed as she remembered something. "We're going to see Dürrenmatt's *The Visit* at the Volksbühne," she said.

"Ah! That's a good choice," Fritz affirmed." What about returning on Sunday for a special tour of East Berlin?" asked Karl.

"Yes! A special personalized custom tour!" Fritz exclaimed with delight, gesturing as well to Kathy, Judy, Molly, and Madeline. The other Germans and Ken applauded the idea and offered to escort the other girls for Sunday sightseeing.

Marlo frowned. "Oh no, I'm leaving Sunday for Stuttgart."

About that time, the others decided to do something else. Marlo, Emily, Karl, and Fritz remained at the Lindenkorso for dinner. Marlo had her first experience eating a German dish, imported by Russian soldiers, called Tartar—raw hamburger with egg, onion, and spices. It tasted better than she expected.

"If you wouldn't mind having us join you for tonight's play, we might be able to get tickets for ourselves," suggested Fritz.

Following supper, they all left for the theater. The fellows were able to obtain tickets for the performance, and they all sat together.

Marlo felt quite relaxed, sitting next to Karl and sharing the theater experience with him. She began to lose her reserve because she thought nothing would come of this new relationship. Soon they would go their separate ways. After the performance, Karl, Fritz, Marlo, and Emily returned to the restaurant on the corner of Unter den Linden and Friedrichstrasse for coffee and cake. They explored in greater depth their respective personal interests, hobbies, and family.

Karl was surprised by the tempo with which this level of sharing occurred, for in his culture, these tokens of growing intimacy usually did not emerge on a first date. This was a new experience for Karl as it was for Marlo. Like Marlo, Karl had no date life to speak of, not even a high school sweetheart of any consequence. What was happening excited him. Adding to the excitement was the mystique of an *American* woman.

As Marlo warmed her hands on the coffee cup, Karl said, "Marlo, why don't you try to get your flight to Stuttgart changed so you can return Sunday? I'd really like to show you around this part of the city. There are so many interesting things to see that fit in with your academic major."

Marlo's eyes met his. The intensity was too much, and she looked down at her coffee and nervously rubbed the rim of the cup with her fingers.

"I . . . I . . . I . . . Ah . . . Yes . . . it would be fun to come back," she said with a trembling voice. "I'll see what I can do." Her eyes swept back up to Karl's face. Her fluttery stomach matched the tingling sensation on the back of Karl's neck. They became so absorbed in each other that the people and surroundings seemed to fade into the distance and the passage of time was unnoticed, even unimportant.

Karl's consciousness suddenly jerked him into the present moment. He glanced at his watch, tossed his head toward Marlo and Emily. "I hate to break this up, but you need to start back to the U-Bahn station before curfew, or you'll have big trouble with the border guards." With his jaw set and neck stiffened, he added sarcastically, "And they can arbitrarily decide not to let you return to this side again."

With uncommon animation, Marlo exclaimed, "Thank you so much for a very enjoyable evening! I'm glad you and Fritz decided to come along!" Emily nodded happily. They laughed.

"I hope we'll see you on Sunday. We'll plan to meet you outside the Lindenkorso at twelve o'clock," Karl said with a sense of reassurance. Fritz agreed.

Together, Fritz and Karl called out, "Auf Wiedersehen!"

"Wiedersehen!" the girls replied in impeccable German. Once Emily and Marlo got past the tense atmosphere of the East German subway station, they became effusive as they recounted their evening of unexpected pleasure. They exchanged intermittent glances and giggled.

"I think you really like Karl," commented Emily. "I saw it in your eyes."

Embarrassed, Marlo looked away. "Well . . . yes . . . Karl seems like a very nice guy."

"Yeah, I think both of 'em are really sweet."

"I *really do* want to return on Sunday," Marlo asserted. Though she didn't say so out loud, Marlo felt she wanted to explore more of Karl, whose self, she observed, was submerged like an iceberg below the ocean's surface.

As they walked back to their dorm, Karl and Fritz laughed and joked. Obviously, they were stimulated by their encounter with the lovely young ladies from the West, from America, from *California*!

"See, what did I tell you, Karl? It did you a lot of good to go out tonight. Look at what you would have missed had you stayed in your room."

"Ha! I do feel so much better. And I do want to see Marlo again."

"Emily and Marlo speak very good German—no foreign accent!"

"Like they've lived here all their lives."

Saturday morning, Marlo called the Fochs family in Stuttgart, with whom she would visit, to see if she could delay her arrival for one day. They were accommodating. When she completed the call, Marlo squealed.

Then she phoned the airline office and changed her flight reservation. Everything was falling into place.

Marlo and Emily went shopping to buy Karl and Fritz some gifts—chocolates, coffee, some West German magazines, and that day's edition of *Die Welt*, a West German newspaper. They were ready for their return visit, and Sunday could not arrive too soon!

Remembering the time it took to cross the border Friday afternoon, Marlo and Emily set out for the subway station earlier in the morning. It was a beautiful sunny but brisk day. They decided to walk, passing the historic Potsdamer Platz as they followed the contour of the Berlin Wall to Checkpoint Charlie at Friedrichstrasse with its formidable barricaded, zigzag thoroughfare between the Western Allied sector and that of the GDR.

On the advice of their West Berlin instructor, Emily and Marlo wore the magazines and newspaper under their clothing since East German law prohibited Western propaganda from entering the country. Because the crisp fall day warranted their wearing heavy coats, Marlo and Emily had plenty of camouflage for the contraband. Even so, the girls were apprehensive as they filed tourist visa papers and complied with other regulations imposed by the GDR customs officers.

As they approached the hotel café, Marlo came to a sudden halt. The blood in her veins seemed to empty from her body. Emily looked on incredulously. Marlo pointed to the street corner. Fritz was standing there alone. The girls greeted Fritz, but Marlo felt empty.

Emily asked Marlo's unspoken question, "Where is Karl?"

"Oh, he just had some things to take care of around the corner," said Fritz. "I'll go get him."

Marlo's body telegraphed a message of relief.

Shortly Fritz arrived with Karl. Marlo conveyed her Stuttgart change of plans. Karl was visibly delighted. Emily and Marlo shared their gifts with the guys.

"We brought you two something else," reported Emily. "Magazines and a newspaper."

"We're wearing them under our clothes, and they're getting pretty scratchy," added Marlo as she wrinkled her nose and frowned.

Emily began to reach up under her coat and her skirt to pull out the printed matter irritating her legs. Fritz lunged forward to prevent Emily from disclosing on a public street what she had smuggled. He clumsily grasped her butt. He pulled away. His face turned red. He started to laugh. The other three chuckled uproariously, sinking to the ground. By the time they had recovered their composure, Fritz was ready to apologize to Emily. Somehow, an apology did not seem to be expected or required.

"It's very risky to reveal such reading material in a public place," Fritz told them.

"If you're caught," Karl added solemnly, "we all might be put in jail."

Marlo and Emily swallowed hard and apologized.

"Well," inquired Emily in an effort to keep a straight face, "is there a women's lavatory nearby where Marlo and I can slip out of these forbidden undergarments?"

"No no no! You don't want to go into a public toilet to do that," insisted Karl. "Remember, there's a washerwoman in there."

The four of them were in a quandary for a few minutes.

"I know," said Karl, "let's go up to my room. You can undress . . . er . . . I mean you can slip the publications out there." Karl's face turned the same shade of red as worn by Fritz a few minutes earlier. The giggles that ensued disarmed the polite reserve that had previously accompanied the four of them.

While in Karl's dorm room, Marlo got interested in the books in his bookcase. He was impressed with her interest. Karl reached to a shelf and pulled out a small volume containing black silhouettes against a white background of distinguished German personages of Goethe's era. It was a popular method of retaining images during that time, a precursor of photography.

"Marlo, I want you to have this book, a gift from me to you," said Karl.

"Oh, thank you, Karl. That is really sweet."

The two couples left the dorm for lunch at the Rathskeller and then packed a lot of sightseeing into the afternoon. It was St. Hedwig's Cathedral and then on to the Pergamonmuseum to see statues and replicas from ancient Greece and Rome. They visited the cemetery in which Bert Brecht, Hegel, and Fichte were buried.

For a change of pace, they went to a music store to pick out some records as a memento of their visit. They took recordings into little booths to hear the music before buying the albums. Marlo selected Ravel's suite *Ma mère l'oye*, which included the composer's renderings of famous fairy tales—"Beauty and the Beast," "The Nightingale," and others. At a deeper level of consciousness, Marlo's choice of music captured her sense of living a fairy-tale experience—just too good to be true.

A chilled darkness fell upon Berlin that evening. The four adventurers dined and played at the Weinachtsmarkt—something like a county fair. Even though Karl was not one for amusement parks, he did find the fun the others were having to be contagious. It wasn't long, however, before the chill factor got to them. True to that country's custom, they made their way to a café to get warm. Over hot drinks, they poured out more personal stories.

Their time together was coming to a close as the clock struck eleven. Karl and Marlo exchanged addresses, phone numbers, and photographs. As they handed these to each other, their hands touched. Karl rested his open hand on Marlo's. Their joined hands found gentle repose on the tabletop. Their eyes met but this time, for a long, deep gaze. No words were spoken. Speech wasn't necessary to convey what they felt and read in each other's eyes—sadness that they would part, and a wistful wondering if they would ever see each other again.

Marlo felt warmed all over as she thought how lucky she was to have met Karl—someone who seemed to care for her as a person, a gentleman. He was so different from the other men Marlo had known in college—either too serious or too glib and superficial. Karl was the first man Marlo had met with whom she felt comfortable being herself and being accepted. The relationship offered her the refreshingly unique mix of being able to talk political philosophy and burst into fun-loving laughter! Exhilarating? Yes! But also a bit frightening. Neither she nor Karl had moved so close to the threshold of intimacy before. In their heart of hearts, they knew that intimacy involves openness and openness can mean vulnerability, and vulnerability is full of risk. Marlo felt most secure when she was in control of her life. Gnawing at her unconscious level of consciousness was the question, *can intimacy and control coexist?*

Karl had awakened new emotions within Marlo. She did not know how much to read into their feelings for each other in this brief encounter complicated by the political reality of their two worlds.

For his part, Karl was in touch with what he intuited as love. His heart sent throbs into all parts of his body. He had not known such tenderness in a relationship. But that was in fierce conflict with the cruel thought that nothing could come of a relationship between an East German and an American. He knew he could not leave East Germany, and surely there would be no future for Marlo in the GDR. Karl was sickened by the insuperable clash of their two worlds. Yet he couldn't help himself. He wanted more of Marlo in his life.

The midnight curfew at the border was oppressively crowding the precious time Marlo and Karl were sharing. How intimidating the clock can be! Like many East-West couples, for whom the Berlin Wall had become a formidable obstacle, Karl and Marlo, together with Emily and Fritz, joined the parade down Friedrichstrasse to the austere border station. The moment of saying farewell was awkward. Karl and Marlo were hopelessly drawn to each other by a force like the gravitational pull of planets. Had there been the slightest provocation, there would have been an embracing kiss. But they were restrained, each waiting for the other's subtle gesture of invitation. Massive energy repressed what they so eagerly wanted but sensed was futile. They fought to conceal their tears.

Emily and Marlo were jolted from the tender parting when the East German border guards abruptly signaled them to step forward to the gate and then raised pointed questions about the record albums clutched in their arms. Checking their money against the currency declarations written on their entry applications earlier that day, a guard saw that money had not been exchanged for the albums.

"Where did you get these albums?" inquired the guard in a gruff tone.

"They're gifts from our friends," replied Marlo.

Fritz explained, "We bought them as gifts."

"Show me the receipts," ordered the guard.

Masking their anger over this unnecessary hassle, Karl and Fritz produced the receipts. The officer studied the slips of paper carefully, handed them back, and motioned to the girls to move through the checkpoint. There was no time left for hugs or kisses. When Marlo and Emily got safely into the Allied sector, they turned and waved to Karl and Fritz. Turning and walking into the darkness was as painful for Karl as it was for Marlo. Neither could express verbally to their companions what they were feeling. Words got caught in the throat. They vanished into the night.

Marlo's study program finished for the semester. She took the train to Stuttgart the next day, where she spent two weeks with a German couple that had sponsored her stay in Germany—Emil and Gert Fochs. She could not take her thoughts away from Karl. She wrote him a note.

Dear Karl,

I arrived safely in Stuttgart. I've been thinking of you and our time together. Thank you for the unforgettably marvelous days we shared. I hope we can meet again sometime before I leave for the United States.

Fondly, Marlo

With a Eurail pass in hand, Marlo spent the next two weeks touring Europe. Staying in youth hostels and traveling by rail made the trip affordable. She was spellbound by the magnificence of cathedrals, palaces, and museums in such awesome venues as Munich, Salzburg, Innsbruck, Zurich, and Vienna before returning to the Fochs' home. When she arrived, two long letters from Karl were waiting for her, followed by a short afterthought in this note:

Dear Marlo,

I was so happy to get your letter! After the Christmas holidays with my family in Meissen, I plan to return to Berlin by New Year's Eve. It would be wonderful to get together. I really want to see you again. Please come to Berlin. We can meet on New Year's Day at our special place—the Lindenkorso.

Better yet, have the Fochs tell you how to take a train to Meissen for Christmas with my family. I can pick you up at the train station. You have my phone number. Yes?

Your friend,
Karl

Marlo's heartbeat caught the excitement surging within. Oh how she wanted to see Karl again. But she remembered how difficult it had been to say good-bye. She wrote—

Karl, I would like to see you again. You are special to me. But my greatest fear is that our relationship has no future. I am not even sure where our relationship is going. It really hurts me to say this, but it would be easier not to see each other again than to prolong the agony of border farewells and a final good-bye. Sorry!

Yours,
Marlo

She wept as she wrote her name and signed the fate of their future. Marlo needed to protect the tender place in her heart, in her whole being, with stoicism. Melancholy eventually invaded that shrine of love and happy memories. *Besides*, she reasoned, *there is no future for an American living in Communist East Germany.*

A devastating war and its aftermath had conspired against such a love affair. Nobody knew that truth any better than Kurt, Eva, and their family.

CHAPTER 5

If devastation and hardship might douse a romantic spark between East and West, a normal life among Germans themselves was untenable. Growing up in the same Meissen neighborhood, Eva and Kurt were childhood sweethearts. Eva's father was a trust officer in the Dresdener Bank. In the same month that Kurt took charge of his parents' grocery store at the age of twenty-two, he and Eva were married. World War II had been waging for a few years, but it did not interfere with life in this quiet, prosperous town on the Elbe River, devoid of military targets.

The full-time operation of the store and the military draft delayed the start of a family. Kurt was finally discovered by the Nazi high command, which then pressed him, an unwilling combatant by nature, into the infantry in the dismal winter of 1944. Eva was left to handle the market alone. Kurt was assigned to the eastern front and quickly found himself a part of a depleted military force with a lack of morale and ordnance reinforcement. Correspondence was haphazard with no visits home for the year that Kurt was on the Russian front. Eva had difficulty coping and was frequently immobilized by depression.

Early in 1945, Kurt was wounded by shrapnel embedded in his left leg resulting from a mortar round exploding near his foxhole. When the news eventually reached Eva, she thought this was a blessing in disguise. He had been moved from the danger of the intense battle zone and put close to Meissen at a Dresden convalescent hospital. But she could not have known that only a few days after his arrival at the hospital, Dresden would undergo its worst siege in history—the heaviest Western Allied bombardment of the war. Although Meissen was only a short train ride away, Eva might just as well have been a thousand kilometers from her lover. Mass confusion, panic, and an evacuation of thousands of citizens would prove to be too great an obstacle for her to make a connection with Kurt. The most she could hope for was that he'd survive.

The week of February 4 had been overcast, bringing showers and snow to the Dresden area. On Sunday, February 11, it cleared. There were rumors that the Allied forces might be planning to take advantage of the improved weather to concentrate a heavy attack on the eastern sector of Germany to hasten the end of the war. Axis soldiers and civilian refugees were retreating from places like Berlin, Leipzig, Poland, and the western Russian border. All of them were vulnerable to being boxed in at the Elbe. By this time, a growing number of Germans, disenchanted with the excesses of the Nazi Third Reich, had organized themselves into an underground movement to cooperate with the Allies in bringing an end to the devastating war. Few seemed to notice the light burning late through the nights of February 11 and 12 in an old Victorian-style house sitting on the hillside overlooking the Elbe and the city, a villa called San Remo. Citizens were trying to prepare for some kind of Allied military offensive, the details of which were still vague. Devout Christians were preparing for Lent, which would begin on Ash Wednesday, February 14.

Meanwhile, farther west across the English Channel, the stage was set for the offensive.

Wednesday, February 14, 0515 hours, on the outskirts of Kimbolton, some sixty miles north of London, Staff Sergeant Shaw stood over the bunk of Captain John Stover, shaking his legs.

"Captain Stover, sir," Shaw whispered. "Are you awake, sir?"

Stover grunted, barely opening his eyes into slits.

"Sir, the squadron commander has called a briefing for 0600. You are on the board for a mission today."

"Uh . . . okay . . . thanks, Shaw." John Stover fought off his drowsiness and dressed. He wondered if it would be Berlin again or some obscure target with low retaliatory risk for a change. Captain Stover was a member of the US Eighth Air Force attached to the 379th bomb group, the Third Air Division. He commanded a crew of his B-17, dubbed Oh Lady Luck—words accompanied by a mechanic's painting of a voluptuous woman rolling snake eyes on the dice on the exterior of the fuselage. The crew already had logged safely two dozen heavy daytime bombing missions over Germany and were due for a furlough. *Lady Luck?* Stover grunted to himself. *No, tough luck!*

In the briefing room, squadron commander Mark Winslow surveyed the stony faces of the pilots, copilots, and bombardiers. "Men," he said in measured words spoken in a somber tone, "the high command in London is pulling out all the stops today. We're mounting an intense offensive designed to break the back of Jerry and end this damn war so we can all go home! Since 2200 hours last night, the Royal Air Force began a massive assault from the Rhine to the Russian border. The First and Third Divisions of our bomb group will be joining forces with the Fifteenth Air Force and the RAF on a mission that will extend over seventy-two hours."

Winslow ceremoniously drew back the curtain to reveal the map of the day's raid. That elicited a chorus of oohs and aahs from the air men.

The commander continued, "As you can see here, the First Division will move across the Rhine at Cologne with secondary targets at Hanover, Hamburg, and Berlin. Your primary target is Dresden. The RAF has completed its night raid with extensive incendiary bombardment. It's hell on the ground, you can be sure of that! Expect some dense smoke over the target area, but the weather report is good with unlimited ceiling. However, you will have to keep your formations tight and follow compass readings carefully when you lose visual contact in the smoke. Your targets in Dresden are the factories and railway yards noted on this map. If the RAF missed any of the bridges over the Elbe, knock them out too. Areas of cultural importance are outlined in these grids here and there in red as usual." Winslow pointed with his baton. Squadron personnel took careful notes. "You must avoid striking those areas," he ordered. "There are valuable art collections housed in the museum, across the plaza in the palace, and the opera house. Posted on the other chart is the information you need on target coordinates and projected winds aloft and at ground level. Any questions?"

Remembering earlier assaults on nearby Leipzig, the division's "crack" bombardier, a member of Stover's crew, spoke up. "Sir, you didn't mention any secondary or tertiary targets for us."

"That's right," responded Winslow. "You have only one set of primary targets. That's it." He tapped the locations on the Dresden map with his pointer. "We're not going to waste our payload on anything else. Dresden is too crucial. You're going to slam the hell out it and get out of there! One more thing. Keep your heads up and eyes wide open. There'll be much more Allied air activity going on simultaneously than ever before. Be alert for sorties going on below and around you. No time for idle chatter on this mission."

"Will we have fighter escort protection?" someone asked.

"Yep. P-51 Mustangs. They'll stay with you until the outskirts of Dresden. That's it."

Stover's attention to the discussion faded as he thought to himself about the gravity of this mission. *How will the dice roll this time for Oh Lady Luck?* The skill of John and his crew earned them the dubious honor of being the lead aircraft in the first squadron of forty planes. Oh Lady Luck carried radar equipment and the crack bombardier. They were susceptible to heavy flak and the target of ME-262 German jet fighters notorious for being light and fast with only fifteen minutes of fuel on board, often landing on a dead stick. The fighters were known to fly into the condensation trail of the bombers, where they could not be seen, fire their rounds of ammunition, and dive. The pathfinder crews always got the brunt of Jerry antiaircraft salvos, but especially the lead and deputy lead planes loaded with the bomb radar device and Mickey operator.

John's thoughts turned to his agricultural valley home near Salinas, California, about which another hometown boy, Steinbeck, wrote in his novels. It was a day late in 1942 that John had enlisted with five of his buddies at the old Salinas air base and was then shipped out for training elsewhere in the states. *But now, Salinas seems so far away . . . so very far away,* he thought wistfully. He had quickly married his high school sweetheart, Margaret. With thousands of other Californians, Stover was shipped out to Lincoln, Nebraska, during one of the bitterest winters on record. Dressed for California weather, many of the fellows died of pneumonia. From Lincoln, Stover was among those sent for some college training at the University of Montana in Missoula, a town of friendly, hospitable homes for servicemen. After three months there, John transferred to preflight training in Santa Ana, California. Then it was off to primary flight school of sixty-five hours in Visalia and basic flight training in Chico. Advance training followed in another California city, Stockton, where John Stover received his wings. He had felt so lucky to have stayed in California while many of his friends were sent off to distant places throughout the States.

While in his deep thought in the briefing room, John recalled how disappointed he was when he got passed over for first pilot. So he and his entire class got shipped off to Kingman, Arizona, for copilots' school. They trained in B-17s. He thought about the early summer days in Kingman, when the temperature was so hot that the plane wheels sunk into the asphalt runway and, on other days, when crews reported to the flight line in their underwear and began putting their clothes on once airborne at fifteen thousand feet! From Kingman, it was back to Lincoln to be sorted into flight crews that were dispatched to Biggs Field in El Paso for training as a crew in flight formations and simulated air attacks. Eventually they found themselves at Camp Kilmer in New Jersey. While some of John's comrades were able to fly to England, he and others took a more leisurely passage on the *Aquatania*. That it was the sister ship to the *Lucitania*, sunk during World War I, did not particularly thrill the men any more than two fish meals served on board each day throughout the entire cruise!

As he continued to sit in the briefing hut, John Stover thought about his group arriving in Stone, England, expecting within two or three days to be sent out on their first mission. Nearly two weeks went by with no assignment! Yet they kept hearing the casualty reports that surely called for immediate replacements. A pilot had become disturbed about it and pressed his inquiry. It turned out that the headquarters staff did not know his crew was at the base! Their papers had fallen behind a filing cabinet! They might well have sat out the war. That thought brought a smile to John's face. He also grinned at the thought that he had made the rank of captain.

John's thoughts turned to the realization that becoming a part of a proficient crew meant they could be sent home after flying only thirty missions instead of thirty-five, because lead squadrons were always the number one target of the enemy. Because the lead crew flew under such intense pressure, they went out only every fourth day instead of flying three consecutive days, resting one.

"Ah-ten-hut!" the sergeant major snapped, jolting Stover's consciousness back into the room. Mark Winslow strode out of the Quonset hut and into the brisk, damp predawn air.

"Dee-smissed!" the sergeant barked. John Stover glanced down at his notebook. During his reverie, he had automatically recorded all the data of the briefing.

On his way to the mess and quartermaster buildings to grab a quick cup of coffee and Danish before picking up his gear for the flight, John passed the hut that served as a chapel. He peered in through a steamed window to see a Catholic priest administering the ashes on the foreheads of devout comrades. Then they would receive the Eucharist.

*I wonder where the Protestant chaplain is. I've been scared before, but this mission is a big one! I don't know . . . there's somethin' spooky about goin' out on a holy day. I don't like it. I sure could use some extra help from the Guy Upstairs. Where in th' hell is my sky pilot? Hmm, maybe I should've gone to Sunday school more often. Maybe I should've paid more attention to God all the time, not jus' when I'm in trouble. Where **is** the chaplain? I could go in there, but I don't know anythin' 'bout Catholics. I wouldn't know what ta do. I'd make a fool of myself. Oh hell! There ain't any time ta find the chaplain now. Man, I sure could use a prayer!* John backed away from the window and rubbed the chilly condensation of his breath from his face. The next thing he knew, he was being swept along in the commotion of the crowd as the fellows dashed to the mess hall for a quick slug of java and the requisition of their parachutes and other gear from the quartermaster.

Oh Lady Luck pointed its nose skyward and left the runway under the full thrust of its engines. John's plane circled above for a while as other planes of the squadron ascended one by one to join the formation. The drone of the squadron could be heard above the fog that shrouded the English Channel that early Ash Wednesday morning.

"Look!" shouted a crewman into his microphone. "Planes at nine o'clock." Crew members fastened their eyes portside to see the RAF returning from their night raid. Typically they flew like a flock of blackbirds, not in formation. The Yanks rolled their wings as the British flew by, receiving an acknowledging aircraft roll in return. Behind Oh Lady Luck and the squadron, the shore of England receded. It would be at least eight hours before they would see the tarmac at Kimbolton again if they were lucky. They climbed to 26,000 feet and leveled off. Air speed was 240 knots.

"Hey! What th' hell's goin' on up there!" screeched a voice into every earphone on board. The crew recognized the high-pitched voice of Steve, the ball turret gunner positioned on the belly of the aircraft.

"Hey," Steve shouted, "why didn'tsha tell me you were gonna take a leak? The piss is splattering all over the face shield! You damn stupid idiot!"

"Oh swell!" replied the bombardier with unmistakable sarcasm.

Stover had more choice words to fill the airwaves.

Whenever anyone had to pee out of the hose, he was required to alert the ball turret gunner, who could swivel the ball in the opposite direction and avoid the splatter of urine obscuring his vision out the window. Now, however, yellow ice formed over the glass—Steve's line of sight. This heightened the anxiety of the crew because the ball was an important defensive gun position.

Stover died a thousand deaths within himself, feeling certain that his plane would be attacked with an immobilized ball turret. They would have to fly the entire mission vulnerable because one stupid jerk forgot and plastered the turret with frozen urine. For endangering the crew and crippling the mission, John pondered, Winslow would surely remove a stripe from the guy's rank and make him clean off the turret shield with a toothbrush, if not his tongue, when they got back to base—if they got back. If the truth be known, he'd clean the base latrines with a toothbrush for a week!

Fortunately for the crew of Oh Lady Luck and the other planes, the first four hours passed without enemy contact. The navigator gave Stover the high sign, and the captain dipped the port wing for a compass heading of north. The other planes followed as the formation tightened, ready for their Dresden approach.

CHAPTER 6

Kurt Mann had undergone surgery for the removal of shrapnel. Despite lingering pain from his wound, he was able to move about. The hospital had been mercifully untouched by the RAF strafing the city the night before. Every able-bodied person was needed to help people get away from the areas of intense heat of fires still burning out of control or to mill through gutted buildings in search of the injured, the dying, and the dead. Kurt had worked his way down to the bank of the Elbe, where thousands of people had fled to keep from burning in the flames darting all about them. He and other soldiers were pulling out the bodies of those who had drowned in the mayhem, including infants and children still protectively cradled in mothers' arms now limp in death. The stench of burned flesh mixed with chemical odors from spent ordnance was unbearable. The horrifying scene made Kurt sick to his stomach. He joined a mournful chorus of vomiting along the river's edge. Dense smoke billowed for miles into the sky.

Even in the midst of human groans of agony and the crumbling of burning buildings, Kurt thought he could hear the drone of approaching aircraft. He stopped his activity for a minute, stood upright, and looked around. *How can we take any more of this?* he exclaimed to himself. "This city is already reduced to rubble," he murmured. Then he tried to shake off the thoughts as he resumed rescue and recovery.

In Altstadt and across the river in the newer sector of Dresden, signals shrieked another warning of an air attack. By this time, there was no safe hiding place. Havoc was caused by people screaming and running in every direction. Kurt decided to stay and continue his gruesome task at the river. He knew there was nowhere to go, no way to avoid what was coming. Kurt resigned himself simply to finish his life doing something humane, spending himself in an act of contrition. *Perhaps this is a way to redeem my part in Hitler's warring madness!* Kurt's thoughts now turned to Eva. He whispered a prayer for her safety. His tall, bulky figure with blue eyes, blond hair, and ruddy complexion was silhouetted against black and grey and flashing red—a ghoulish specter.

CHAPTER 7

As Oh Lady Luck approached the target area, Stover looked down. *Well, there goes all that Dresden china . . . Wow! What destruction . . . Why are we here? Isn't this overdoing it?* Then, John and his crew were into thick soup. The smoke was worse than clouds. Heat rising from below caused turbulence. They bounced all over hell's half acre in the sky. The smell of smoke filled the fuselage. As Oh Lady Luck made its bombing raid in concert with the other planes, confusion broke out in the skies. Suddenly another B-17 swept across the path of Oh Lady Luck, running off its intended compass heading and altitude. Stover's heart took a flying leap for his throat. His copilot vomited.

Bart, the nose gunner, with one bodily jerk, puked. "Oh no!" he cried out. "I pissed and shit in my pants. Dammit! I'm a gawd awful mess."

Stover said, "Easy does it, kid. Yer not the first ta lose it. Probably not the last. Yer goin' ta be okay. Here, mop up with this towel."

The pilots were into instrument flying for sure. Nothing was visible now, not even the sight of the miniature puffs of explosions below, which somehow made bombing raids seem like only a game. Within twenty minutes, the lead squadron had spent its cargo over the targets and was homeward bound for a safe landing at Kimbolton.

One by one, crew members reported to Stover any injuries of personnel and signs of damage sustained by the aircraft. Except for bumps and bruises from the turbulence, the crew had escaped serious bodily harm or, worse, death. A piece of the plane's stabilizer had sheared off, causing some pitching in flight back to England. The belly gunner continued to stare at his frosted window in dismay. This was one rare mission in which his guns, like the other machine guns on board, were cold and silent.

CHAPTER 8

The inferno below was unspeakable. It defied description. Kurt had no words to express his thoughts or characterize his experience. And perhaps it was just as well. He didn't think it was something in one's war stories to tell children and grandchildren should he even survive to produce a progeny. All through Ash Wednesday, 4,000 tons of explosives rained on Dresden, emptied from the bowels of 1,400 bombers.

Blackened tears streaked down Kurt's face as he stood transfixed. He couldn't even weep, for his throat was constricted and aching. *How ironic that this great, beautiful city of old Saxony should be reduced to smoldering embers on this holy day!*

Many times in its history, Dresden had burned in fires and had been plundered in wars. Yet she had been rebuilt, and her ancient splendor had been restored. Maybe her tough, determined sense of history and cultural nobility would once again enable this phoenix to rise from the ashes. Not far from where Kurt was standing was the Dresden palace in shambles. Yet across the boulevard and theater plaza, the opera house and Zwinger art gallery stood intact, with only the outer walls blackened by incendiary explosions. Miraculously, the thirteenth-century stone Augustus Bridge, linking the old and new city centers, had survived the bombing. Kurt was grateful that they had been spared. *God, I hope this means the demise of the Nazis!* He desperately wondered about Eva's well-being. He choked on his sobs. Knowing her emotional state, Kurt was especially concerned about her frame of mind.

The Allied aerial assault was relentless. It was Friday before the reign of terror ended. Early that Friday morning, another soldier standing near Kurt flailed his arms wildly, pointing alternately toward the collapsing Catholic cathedral and the Lutheran Frauenkirche, once prominent on the skyline of Altstadt—the city's older sector. He cried out, "Look! Look! Even God has deserted us . . . even God!" Kurt trained his eyes on those landmarks and wept.

Eight thousand planes had passed over the city. By the weekend, it became clear that the firestorm had consumed everything organic. Tens of thousands of lives had been snuffed out. Many thousands more had been maimed and left homeless. The blood-washed Elbe was infested with ghosts. Never again would a Dresdener bathe or swim in its waters out of remembrance of what happened there and respect for its innocent victims.

Kurt looked down at his feet. There was the body of a girl, maybe eight or nine years of age, he had pulled out of the Elbe. He sat down on the ground next to her. His face was blistered and blackened and wet with sweat and tears. He gently took the girl's stiffened hand and studied her pallid face, which exhibited an eerie sense of now-deserved eternal peace.

Softly he spoke to her, "Look at us, my little one, look at us! Who's better off, huh? You or us, the living dead?"

He looked away for a moment. Shook his head. He swallowed hard, then turned to the girl and continued, "Is this our sin against London and Coventry coming home to roost?"

Kurt was quiet for a moment. He just looked at the girl as if they had been friends for a long time. He thought of the wedding she would never have, the children to whom she'd never give birth.

"What kind of madness is this?" he asked her. "We revolt against our better nature, and these fires of hell make toast of the good and the bad . . . the just and the unjust. It's . . . savage . . ." His voice trailed off. *I hope the burial detail lays her to her proper rest.* He wiped his face, eased himself up on his feet, and stumbled off to Meissen to see if his home and store were recognizable and if Eva was okay.

From a distant hillside, he paused and looked back at Dresden. He didn't recognize it. He had a flashback from his early youth of a Basque town, Guernica, in northern Spain. He remembered a newspaper photo of that town left in ruins after three and a half hours of cruel, senseless bombing by the German Luftwaffe on April 26, 1937, at the request of General Franco and his rebel forces. Kurt did not know that an outraged Pablo Picasso, a Spanish expatriate, would form on canvas a ghastly depiction of that event, perhaps not unlike the conflagration along the Elbe.

CHAPTER 9

By a stroke of good fortune, Kurt, Eva, their home, and their store survived the tormenting nightmare days of the war. They started their family, and after one miscarriage, they gave birth to Karl and, six years later, Albert.

The war may have been over but not the tribulations of most East Germans, who, like the Manns, embraced decency, peace, and freedom. Now they were a part of a Communist block behind what Winston Churchill dubbed the Iron Curtain.

Karl shared his parents' sensibilities. From age ten, Karl was exposed in the school system to Communist ideology and political policies. These were tempered by what visiting relatives from West Germany would have to say about their political situation and lifestyle in the West. Eva and Kurt were very much aware that many of their GDR countrymen were fleeing to the West—a major reason for the shortage in the labor force. Even with the importation of cheap labor from neighboring Eastern European nations, the government was abysmally slow in rebuilding highways, public housing, and commercial buildings, which took nearly four decades after the war to complete. One of Dresden's landmarks, the eighteenth-century Baroque Frauenkirche (The Church of Our Lady), where Johann Sebastian Bach had once played the organ, still remained in ruins, not expected to be restored anytime soon. But on that site, a statue of Martin Luther, sixteenth-century Protestant reformer, stood intact as a silent sentinel over the unavoidable reminder of war's horrific barbarism.

Adolescent boys like Karl were recruited for Young Pioneers in which they were taught many forms of physical fitness, manual dexterity, plus a generous dose of Communist principles.

"Now, the gun you hold in your hands is for the peace of the world," the Young Pioneers instructor told the assembled youth. "It is necessary to fight against those who try to destroy our beautiful country. Especially must we be vigilant about the bad influence of imperialist West Germany and the United States." Karl was taught over and over that the Soviets were good and trusted friends of East Germany.

Prior to the summer of 1961, Kurt and Eva frequently talked of leaving the country. Kurt's friend Ernst Hofmeister, an industrialist after the war, made frequent trips to West Germany on business.

"Kurt, I'm leaving for Berlin on Monday. Give me a few more of your belongings to put in my suitcase and trunk. I'll stash them in my friend's warehouse in West Berlin."

"A couple more trips and we'll have enough stored over there to leave and start a new life," Kurt replied with a sigh.

Two weeks later, the Manns met with Ernst and Anne Hofmeister to finalize plans to escape to West Germany.

"Are the two of you satisfied that you have enough personal belongings in West Berlin to establish yourselves and your sons there?" Ernst asked.

"Of course," Kurt said. "I'm waiting to hear from my sister. She's considering taking over the store for us."

Eva began to shift her feet from side to side, signaling to Kurt her growing nervousness.

"All right then, let's plan to make our move next Monday. I'm due to make another business trip to Berlin. You know, I've gotten to know the border guards on duty Monday mornings. Usually they don't check my vehicle or luggage. Sometime ago, the officers allowed Anne to accompany me. I'm hoping they'll let us leave the GDR together once again. I think I've developed a good level of trust."

"Well, what if there are different guards this time?" Eva asked anxiously. "What if they won't let Anne leave with you? What if they search your car?"

"I can't say there's no risk involved. But it's worth the risk, isn't it?"

Eva's face was contorted. She was not convinced.

"Look, I can't remember the last time the guards searched my van and luggage! I think it's a low risk, I really do."

After dinner, the two men delved into strategies to make it safely across the border. The discussion made Eva visibly nervous. She couldn't take it any longer. She hastily gathered up the supper dishes and shuffled into the kitchen. Her elbow hit the kitchen door, jarring loose several plates and cups. They fell to the floor with a loud crash, breaking into many pieces. Eva shook all over and cried out. She ran into the bedroom and slammed the door.

Kurt excused himself and went to her. She was lying on the bed. Her face was buried in a pillow. He sat beside her, gently rubbing her back and shoulders as he often did when he found her tense and distraught. He didn't say a word. He only sat there, massaging her tight muscles.

When Eva's sobbing subsided, she said in a faint voice, "Oh, Kurt . . . I can't . . . I can't do it."

"Shh . . . quiet, my dear."

"Ohhh . . . it won't work . . . I *know* it, I *know* it! What will become of us . . . our family? We'll lose everything."

"Eva, Eva, it *will* work! We won't take unnecessary chances, certainly not with Karl and Albert."

Eva's whole body tensed up again. She began to shake uncontrollably. Kurt rubbed her neck and head. That helped some.

"Kurt, you *know* how important it is for me to feel secure—"

"Yes, my love, I know, I know," he interrupted. "And we will find a new security, a *better* security in the West."

"But I love our home here, Kurt. It's all we've known from our childhood."

"And so do I, Eva. But you know, things have changed. Life here is not the same as we've known it. And months ago you agreed—"

"That was months ago!" she retorted. "I've changed my mind. I *don't* want to go . . . Do you hear me, Kurt? I *do not* want to go!"

Eva began to sob again. Kurt looked on, taking a deep breath and slowly exhaling. He didn't know what to say.

With resignation in her voice, she said, "You go, Kurt, you go . . . I can't . . . I won't."

He patted her on the shoulder. "Get some rest. We can talk more about this later. Perhaps we don't need to make any moves right away." He knew he couldn't leave her behind. And what about the boys?

He returned to their house guests. "I think we need more time," he told them with some hesitation. Kurt added thoughtfully, "You know Eva, how upset she can get."

"Kurt, we understand," replied Anne. Turning to her husband, "Perhaps we'd better go." Pausing at the door, Ernst said, "Give our regards to Eva and our thanks for the delicious meal. I must say, her apple strudel with that secret recipe sauce is the best in Saxony!" Grasping Kurt's arm, he added, "I'll get in touch with you later. Auf Wiedersehen."

That was the end of that. To preserve Eva's peace of mind, the plan was scuttled. Eva spent the first two weeks of July in bed, recovering from nervous exhaustion.

On August 10, East Germany's leader, Walter Ulbricht, announced that new measures might be enforced to halt the flow of refugees and put pressure on East Berliners not to work in the western sector of the city. In spite of that day's rainy weather, 1,709 refugees fled to the West Berlin reception center. That brought the total for the first ten days of August to 15,041.

At a time when East Germans were leaving at the rate of one a minute, USSR premier Khrushchev ordered Marshal Ivan S. Konev and twenty Soviet army divisions into the tense, divided city.

Then came a stunning news report:

> Dateline: Berlin, Sunday, August 13, 1961—East Germany closed the border early today between East and West Berlin. East German soldiers stood guard at the Brandenburg Gate, the main crossing point between the two sectors. East Berlin officials banned its citizens from holding jobs in the other zone, affecting some 53,000 East Berliners who commute daily to jobs in the western sector.

The Pravda press in Moscow contended that the German Democratic Republic had closed its border to West Berlin to protect the Communist countries from neo-Nazi attacks spurred by NATO. Any hope for the Mann family to make a new life for itself in the West was now shattered.

That reality was even more pronounced when, on Friday, August 18, news came that East German officials had erected a five-feet-high concrete-block wall, sealing off the sectors from Reinechendorf southeast to Neukoelln.

Of little interest to Europeans locked in the clutches of a not-so-Cold War with the Soviets, 37,840 fans set a record for the largest night crowd in Cleveland to see the Yankees' new sluggers, Mantle and Maris, make more gains on Babe Ruth's home run record. Neither could get one over *this* wall as the two superstars went hitless and the Indians emerged victorious. The scoreboard read five to one. The following day, a *New York Times* headline read the following: "Judge Learned Hand Dies; on US Bench 52 Years, a Defender of Freedom against Extremists of Left and Right." He was eighty-nine. What irony to juxtapose seemingly isolated, unrelated events on both sides of the Atlantic!

The Berlin Wall created a peculiar kind of chaos on Harzerstrasse. Everything north of that street was in Communist-ruled East Berlin. But the street itself and sidewalks were in West Berlin. The people living along the north side had the best of both worlds, their doors opening to the bounteous life of the West. However, with the wall came a number of grim workmen nailing shut every door on Harzerstrasse with brick walls put inside the doors. The ends of three side streets leading into Herzerstrasse were walled off. The several hundred people living there in a four-story apartment building were consigned to the restrictions of life in the East. While a remote town like Meissen was hardly affected by the Berlin events of that week, the Mann family was sullen. Procrastination became the grave in which opportunity was buried.

Karl's dream was to become a doctor. But reports about restricted applications to professional schools of any kind led to discouragement. The government needed to rebuild a depleted workforce. More young men were needed in skilled and nonskilled labor to repair dilapidated infrastructure throughout East Germany but cities like Berlin and Dresden in particular. With stepped-up aggressions in Vietnam, young East Germans were being conscripted for military service. Many of them were sent to Vietnam to provide strategic support for the North Vietnamese.

Following a year of basic medical training, Karl took a job as an orderly at a Dresden mental hospital. Hidden away in that setting made it possible for Karl to escape the military draft and provided him with a useful résumé for an acceptable application to the medical college at Humboldt University in Berlin. Almost immediately he began to see the differences between East and West from the unique vantage point of that divided city. From Western German and BBC radio broadcasts, from simple observations, and from common sense, Karl concluded that life was better in the West, just like his relatives had said in earlier days before the wall. Wherever he walked through East Berlin, Karl could see limitations to his freedom and that of others. There was the imposing wall itself with lookout gun towers. The streetcar had to come to a stop some distance from the border and be turned around even though one's destination was still several blocks away. A new experience. He absorbed it. There would be more disquieting revelations to test his sense of hope, his patience, his resolve.

CHAPTER 10

Marlo somewhat reluctantly joined Emil and Gert Fochs for a Christmas Eve observance at a nearby church. During the quiet periods of the candlelight service, she entertained second thoughts about what she had written to Karl and became totally preoccupied with her desire to see him again. When she returned to the Fochs' home, Marlo immediately went to her room and pulled a map of Germany out of her suitcase. She opened it to see how far away Meissen was from Stuttgart. Gert Fochs walked by Marlo's open door and observed Marlo for a moment.

"Planning another trip, Marlo?" she asked.

"Hmm, I was just curious to see how far away Meissen is from here."

"My dear girl, you know that Meissen is in *East* Germany, well beyond the wall!" Gert exclaimed. "It's not as simple as your day trips into East Berlin."

Marlo nodded with a smile that was unmistakably romantic.

Gert returned the smile. No further questions were necessary.

Marlo checked her Eurail pass. It was due to expire on December 28.

"Marlo dear, why don't you just go!"

Marlo broke into a broad smile and threw her arms around Gert. "Thank you, oh, thank you, Mrs. Fochs!"

Christmas morning, Marlo phoned the railroad passenger office to inquire about visa requirement to travel into the German Democratic Republic for an overnight stay.

"No restrictions," was the agent's reply.

Marlo quickly dispatched a telegram to Karl:

Forget my last letter. Will arrive in Meissen by train 7:00 a.m. Marlo.

She threw a few things into her suitcase, anticipating an overnight stay. After supper, the Fochs drove Marlo to the railway station. The train rolled down the tracks on time, taking Marlo on an impromptu long journey to Karl deep into Communist country.

As she settled in her compartment, Marlo couldn't believe what she was doing. Since her high school days in California, she had not been known for being adventurous. Most people who knew her would say she was demure.

The shrieking train whistle announced an approach to a populated area and one of the many stops along the route. Marlo wiped the condensation from the window to take a look at her surroundings. A sign spelled Hof, the last West German town close to the GDR border.

Meanwhile, the Mann family had no sooner gotten seated around the table for Christmas evening supper than the doorbell rang. Kurt took the stairs down into the darkened courtyard and the entrance gate next to the storefront. He returned to the dining room, waving a telegram.

"Karl, this is for you!"

"Oh!" exclaimed Karl with surprise.

Karl opened it, and his facial expression alternated from delight to bewilderment. His fair complexion turned rosy.

The family looked on expectantly, waiting for some revelation.

"Well, Karl, who is it from?" quizzed Albert.

"Ah, it's from Marlo Farrell, an American student I met in Berlin last month."

"Oh-ho!" his father exclaimed. "You never told us about her!"

"Well, we only spent two days together. Then she went to Stuttgart. We corresponded. I never expected to see her in Meissen!" Karl looked again at the short message, trying to be certain he was reading it right.

"She is coming here?" Eva exclaimed.

Shrugging his shoulders, Karl looked on in astonishment. His pulse quickened at the thought of seeing her again. *What a Christmas present this will be!*

Albert winked at his brother. "That must be *some* lady friend!"

Karl tilted his head to one side and grinned.

Kurt and Eva stared at each other in disbelief.

CHAPTER 11

Marlo was excited as the train pulled into Hof. West German officers came through the passenger cars filled to capacity with folks exuding the holiday spirit of festivity.

"May I see your visa, please?" an officer asked her.

"What visa?"

"Anyone going to the German Democratic Republic must have a visa."

"But I don't have one. I was told by a railroad agent in Stuttgart I would not need one since I'm a foreign student."

"You were misinformed. But you may stay on the train. Sometimes the East German border guards will make an exception. And this *is* a holiday."

By this time, Marlo's stomach was churning. The train began to move again but very slowly through the border area until it came to rest at the East German station of Gutenfürst. Marlo looked out of the window to see a line of starched soldiers with grim, stony faces—a stark contradiction to the spirit of that night in which the universe itself continued its joyous carol song. Not only was Marlo's stomach still churning, but her adrenalin was also pumping fiercely through her body.

"Your visa!" said a voice sharply from behind Marlo. It was not the kind of sound one would associate with the making of exceptions, holiday or not!

Marlo turned to see an officer, whose countenance appeared austere, glaring at her.

Marlo's seatmate, a matronly Frau Tillman, looked on sympathetically.

"I do not have a visa. I was told by a railroad agent in Stuttgart I would not need one. Here is my passport."

"Where are you going?" the officer asked dryly.

"To Meissen to visit friends."

"You must deboard the train."

"Will I be able to get back on the train before it leaves?"

"That is unlikely, but possible." He gestured for her to leave.

In dismay, Marlo quickly gathered her things. She pulled out two packages she had wanted to give to Karl as Christmas gifts and handed them to Mrs. Tillman, who was also en route to Meissen.

"May I ask a favor of you?" Marlo asked in perfect German.

Frau Tillman nodded.

"Would you please give these to Mr. Karl Mann, who will be waiting for me at the Meissen train station?" Marlo pleaded.

"Of course I will," the lady assured her.

"Thank you so very much!" Marlo described Karl so the lady would be able to identify him. "Please tell him that I had to leave the train and that I hope to get on another as soon as I can get the visa situation cleared up. I will try to phone him when I arrive."

Stepping from the overheated train into the bitter cold of the snowy winter scene was like a slap in the face. Marlo glanced at her watch and checked it against the time registered on the station clock. It was two o'clock in the morning. She bundled herself up tightly and wrapped her thoughts around the fond hope that she would soon be back on the train once the misunderstanding about the visa got resolved.

Marlo looked around. There didn't seem to be a town or village nearby. Gutenfürst was apparently the name of the border custom control station. Hof was the town some distance from the border. It seemed to set East German authorities at ease not to have people living too close to the border.

"Please step in there," a guard pointed to a little hut next to the office building.

It was certainly nothing more than a *hut*, furnished with a small wooden table and two wooden straight-backed chairs. However, the room offered a welcome relief from the icy wind. A few minutes later, an officer came and guided Marlo into the office where she was confronted by a female border guard in uniform. Marlo thought she could fit the caricature of the hard-line Communist interrogator depicted in films. The woman's severe features were complemented by an angular frame and jutting jaw. Her unbending manner was soon evident in her line of questioning.

"Why do you want to visit East Germany?"

"To visit friends for Christmas." Marlo carefully measured her words.

"What is your destination?"

"Meissen."

"Have you visited our country before?" The woman leafed through the pages of Marlo's passport, apparently looking for a GDR visa stamp.

"Yes. I was granted a tourist visa—you know, for twenty-four hours—in East Berlin."

"Who are you meeting in Meissen?"

"Mr. Karl Mann."

"Is he related to you?"

"No, he is a friend."

"How did you meet Mr. Mann?"

Marlo explained how they had met, hoping that information might encourage the authorities to give her permission to continue her journey. She was also afraid that she might get Karl into trouble. The atmosphere seemed so adversarial.

"Is there any possibility that, even if the person I want to see is not related to me, I might be allowed to visit him?"

"I cannot say for certain. We must have complete names and addresses first, and then you will have to pay a filing fee in West German marks so we can telephone Meissen authorities to verify your information."

Marlo filled out the forms that expected the applicant to know even such details as the exact age and employment of all the members of the household to be visited. She was curious about the guard's need to have payment in West German marks. *Oh yes, West German marks are of greater value than East German marks. Of course!*

"Remain seated here," ordered the woman. "An answer will be forthcoming. You *do* realize the hour of the night. I do not know if I will be able to reach the proper authorities at this hour." The woman returned to her desk to review the forms Marlo had filled out.

Marlo kept looking at her watch nervously and glancing out the window of the hut to see if the train was still there. The border guards were beginning to disembark from the cars. It appeared the train would be leaving soon. Screwing up her courage, Marlo stepped up to the counter and asked, "Please, may I have my visa now so I can get back on the train before—"

"I have only now placed a phone call. There is no official word yet," she snapped. "You must wait!"

There was the inevitable hiss of steam, the familiar rhythmic chug, and a shrill whistle. Marlo was close to tears as she watched the train slowly pull away from the station. She studied a posted train schedule and was relieved to see that the next train would arrive in less than an hour. But her joy faded as she came to the gradual realization that the next train would be traveling in the opposite direction. An east-bound train was not expected until late that morning.

An hour passed, and the west-bound train had come and gone before the woman in charge returned to announce, "Your visa application has been denied. You will have to return to the West."

"But my friend is expecting me!" Marlo asserted with a trembling voice. "Isn't there any other way I can get to Meissen?"

After a long pause, the woman remarked, "There is one way. You can go through the German Democratic Travel Bureau."

"Will it be open today?" Marlo asked, knowing that December 26 is a legal holiday in Germany.

"It is always open."

"I see there isn't another train to Hof for *four hours*. Is there some way I can get back there before the next scheduled train arrives?"

"Perhaps." The woman, now beginning to admire Marlo's persistence, disappeared into another room.

Marlo tried to doze on the armless straight-backed chair without success. She tilted her head against the wall, which was fine for a little while until her neck and shoulders began to ache. It was difficult to nap when her mind was so busy wrestling with the obstacles being erected in her path.

Thirty minutes later, the woman returned. With a faint smile, she said, "A train is coming in right now that you may board."

"You mean I can go to Meissen after all?"

"No, no! Hurry up and get out there and get on that train! It will take you to Hof."

Marlo Farrell rushed out of the building and found the train.

"But . . . that's a *freight* train!" she gasped. Nevertheless, she was a young woman on a mission and was not to be deterred.

She asked the engineer for a ride to Hof. He looked puzzled and cast his eyes toward the hut. The woman guard, now standing on the platform, nodded.

The heavyset old man with a scruffy gray beard was seated in the cab of the engine. He helped her up into the cab. It was an awkward climb in her slim A-line skirt! The engineer was gentle and kind, providing good company on the short hop across the border. His regional dialect was difficult for Marlo to understand, but he seemed sympathetic when Marlo told him her story.

"Love will find a way," he assured her and wished her luck as he helped her down out of the engine compartment and pointed her in the direction of the West German train station passenger platform. "They can tell you where to find the nearest travel bureau."

"Thank you very much. You have been so kind."

"Not at all, my little one," he replied, doffing his cap. "This is the least I can do to help. I would turn this train around and take you nonstop to Meissen if I could!" They waved their good-byes.

The West German guard Marlo encountered in the train station was not at all encouraging. "I think your best move is to return to Stuttgart," he contended. Other guards standing nearby nodded in agreement.

"But the East German officer at the border told me there is a way I can get to Meissen through a travel bureau."

"I suppose you can try," said another guard. "Schmidt's Travel Bureau here in town might be able to help you." He took her to a city map affixed to the wall and pointed to the location.

Marlo hastily sketched out directions on a piece of paper. Turning to one of the guards, she asked, "Would you please look after my suitcase while I'm at the travel bureau?" He consented.

She walked into town. She found Schmidt's. The sign on the door stated eight o'clock as the opening time. Marlo had a forty-five-minute wait. By eight fifteen, the bureau office still had not opened. She approached a passerby to make an inquiry.

"Oh, it's not open today," said the stranger. "Today is a holiday, you know."

Once again Marlo found her hopes hanging on the end of a frayed thread. But she had gone too far to give up. She returned to the train depot. A new shift of guards was on duty. These men seemed much more friendly and responsive.

"That lady at Gutenfürst must have meant the travel bureau at the autobahn border crossing," one of them said. "I believe it is open all the time."

"How do I get there?"

"A taxi," someone suggested.

"Oh dear, is it *that* far? I haven't much money!"

"There is a bus that goes that way," another guard said. "The driver can drop you off near there if you ask him."

The bus Marlo was to take stopped at the depot at nine o'clock. She was relieved to hear the bus driver tell her that his route took him near the autobahn border customs control station. He was not optimistic about her getting across the border.

"It's easier to swim from France to England than to get from here to the GDR!" he quipped. "Why didn't you go to Berlin? The border-crossing regulations are more lax there."

"I'm beginning to ask myself that same question!"

The driver brought the bus to the nearest parking area at customs control, which had a nearby road café, currency-exchange office, public toilets, fueling station, and travel bureau. "Good luck," he said, "but I may see you again when I return to this location in about an hour."

Marlo walked toward the complex of buildings at roadside. She entered the travel bureau. The young man behind the counter informed Marlo, "You must obtain your visa for the GDR on the other side of the border crossing. The East Germans have a travel office like this one. I will make a telephone call to confirm what I have told you."

Marlo waited a few minutes until he completed the call.

"Yes, you can obtain a GDR visa from their bureau. I was told that non-Germans are allowed in on a special tourist visa all the time. Now, it is a bit of a walk. Let me ask a motorist to give you a ride." He succeeded.

The ride was fortuitous, for the distance to the GDR customs control was a kilometer or so down the road with the usual zigzag roadblocks along the way, which would have been hazardous for anyone on foot in the midst of weaving motor vehicles on a single narrow lane . . . She noted the manned gun towers behind barbed-wire fences at intervals along the way. Obviously, they were in East German territory. At the border entrance,

Marlo thanked the people who gave her a ride, and she entered the travel bureau.

An East German woman behind the desk was a refreshing contrast to her Gutenfürst counterpart. She was portly and congenial with a kind voice and manner. Marlo felt immediately at ease. When the woman heard Marlo's story, she remarked, "But of course, I am sure we can help you."

Discovering that Marlo had little money, the lady took it upon herself to assist this American student as much as she could.

"Let's see . . . this will be for the bus fare to Plauen . . . and this is for the train to Meissen . . . and this amount is for your entry visa. Maybe since you have friends there, we can work it out so that you only need to pay for the hotel in advance and not the pre-set amount for your meals."

"A hotel?"

"That is correct."

"But I'm sure my friends will have me stay in their home."

"I am sorry, Ms. Farrell, but that is not possible. You see, government regulations require that in order to enter the country and remain overnight, you must have a hotel reservation."

The woman called the Meissen connection to inquire about a reasonably priced room at a local hotel. In her own mind, Marlo concluded that this requirement was a method by which the government could extract from tourists those valuable West German marks to beef up the economy and also monitor the movement of foreigners. Entry and exit visas were contingent upon such local arrangements. Failure to comply brought stiff fines.

"Ms. Farrell," the clerk reported, "everything is in order. Here is your entrance visa. You must report to the Meissen police station to receive your exit visa. Here is the name and address of your hotel."

Marlo was unbelievably overjoyed at this turn of events. "Oh, *thank you!*"

CHAPTER 12

Many more hours had passed from the time of Marlo's departure from Stuttgart and now from Plauen to her arrival in Meissen. The railroad tracks carried the train over the Elbe River to the depot on the east bank of the river, which glistened beautifully in the moonlight at dusk.

Marlo ran to the nearest public telephone and called the Mann residence.

"Marlo!" exclaimed Karl, who answered the phone before it could ring a second time. "Is that really you? Where are you?"

"I'm here, in Meissen. My train just arrived."

"Stay right there. I'll pick you up in a few minutes."

Marlo walked out onto the main entrance porch and moved toward the river side of the railing. Her eye caught the magnificence of the palace and cathedral on a hilltop across the river silhouetted against the moonlit sky. The picturesque view gave her a sense of tranquility at last.

Karl sped his father's car into the depot parking lot like a racing driver crossing the finish line. As he swerved into a parking space, he spotted Marlo's profile, motionless, as if in a trance. *Ah, what soft beauty she brings.* He lingered a moment in the car, feasting his eyes upon her.

Then he climbed out of the car and ran up the steps, calling out to her. Heat shot through his body as if a bomb had exploded within him. Marlo turned sharply in his direction. Her face was aglow as she ran toward Karl. They embraced, fairly melting into each other's body.

"This is such a nice Christmas surprise!" Karl exclaimed, looking deep into her eyes. "I thought I would never see you again."

Once again, they clung in a rapt embrace. "Oh, I was beginning to think I'd never make it . . . so many obstacles along the way," she said softly in his ear.

Karl stepped back slowly, taking her hands. The moisture in their eyes sparkled like moonbeams. His lips began to brush lightly across her cheek and forehead and eyelids and finally met her lips. Their bodies felt as though they had merged into one. For both of them, this was a new experience, an ecstatic feeling. They were absolutely oblivious to the chill night air.

Arm in arm, they strolled to the car. They drove along the river and took the bridge that offered a scenic approach to the town hall.

"Karl, did a lady on this morning's train find you and explain my situation?"

"Yes. Frankly, I wasn't too surprised. That's pretty common."

"Did the lady give you anything?"

"Oh yes! She gave me two packages. I haven't opened them. Thank you, Marlo." He squeezed her hand.

"I hope all of this hasn't inconvenienced your family."

"Well, no. But my parents were a little unhappy with me for not joining the family for our traditional Christmas celebration at my grandparent's house."

"Oh, I'm so sorry, Karl."

"No, no! I wanted to stay by the phone. I left only two times to meet trains from the West. I really didn't expect you to be on a train that originated in the GDR."

They drove directly to his grandparent's home to join the family in their festivities. They gave Marlo a warm reception. They provided typical German hospitality—a hearty meal with several kinds of meat, vegetables, salads, and traditional cakes that they had delayed for her arrival.

"Ms. Farrell, do tell us about your trip," said Eva Mann.

Marlo recounted every detail of the journey. They were astonished and apologetic. They were not naive about the unpredictability of East German policies and procedures. They had heard many such tales as Marlo shared.

It was a little after ten o'clock when Kurt suggested that Marlo be taken to her hotel. "Surely you must be very tired after all that has happened," he said. Her heightened excitement neutralized any exhaustion.

Karl went into the hotel with Marlo to be sure the accommodations were proper. The management indeed had a record of her name and reservation. The government was very efficient.

Karl carried her luggage up two flights of stairs to her room at the end of a darkened corridor. Getting ready to leave, he said, "I'm so glad you are here, Marlo. Have a good rest. I'll pick you up in the morning about nine o'clock." She nodded. "We'll go to my parent's place for breakfast."

He gave her a tender kiss, into which Marlo gracefully leaned. She stood motionless for a moment, watching Karl until he vanished out of sight. She found her room in the quaint old inn to be spartan and clean yet comfortable.

CHAPTER 13

The next few days for Marlo were overflowing with joyful events in Karl's company. The elder Mann was influential in getting Marlo's visa expiration date extended.

Marlo and Karl walked around the older section of the city, visiting the city hall, museum, library, and Albrechtsburg Castle and cathedral in the heights. The castle's great fifteenth-century towers and multiform vaults of its mammoth halls impressed Marlo. The porcelain factory, though, was a real treat.

"My parents own an expensive set of Dresden china they acquired on a trip to Germany years ago," commented Marlo. "They used it only on very special occasions."

"Expensive? Oh yes! Marlo, I know some people call it *Dresden* china, but it's more proper to call it *Meissen* china."

"Oh. Okay," she said, raising her eyebrows with a pert smile.

The factory showroom recapitulated the history of manufacturing from its inception in 1710 and told the fascinating story of how Johann Friedrich Böttger discovered the formula for hard-paste porcelain using, of all things, wig powder!

"These works of art are breathtaking!" Marlo exclaimed.

Although usually closed during the winter season, the Meissen china demonstration room was open and operating. The two of them, virtually the only observers present, watched the glob of kaolin being shaped on a potter's wheel and observing a completed form of a vase being hand-painted and placed in the furnace for baking.

Marlo could not help but draw from that an analogy of how her own life seemed to have been molded of late, which surely included a trial of circumstances that had to be something like fire in a furnace! *If only it would all work out like the beautiful finished product resting on a pedestal before my eyes.*

Another day of sightseeing found Karl and Marlo in Dresden. Walks through Zwinger and Semper's Gallery were delightful as were occasional pauses in coffee shops to keep warm and talk about their deepening affection for each other. They took a streetcar out of the city to one of Dresden's famous attractions—the Pillnitz Castle, set in the midst of expansive gardens. The winter cold welcomed bright sunshine and deep-blue sky as they walked through the deserted snow-laden gardens and frosted tree branches. They stopped in front of the remarkable centuries-old camellia tree, shrouded under its huge protective canopy. They looked intently into each other's eyes. Words were unnecessary.

Karl took Marlo by the hand and escorted her to a secluded reflection pond surrounded by trees of every sort from different parts of the world—some evergreen and some deciduous. They sat on a bench next to a pond lightly sprinkled with snow. Above them was a linden tree with a few remaining dainty leaves on a branch. One fluttered down and rested on Marlo's scarf tucked around her neck. Karl reached out and gently picked it up and held it between them, twisting the stem back and forth with his thumb and forefinger. The leaf came alive as if dancing a polka. Marlo began vocalizing a musical accompaniment. Before long, they were laughing wildly at this spontaneous gesture.

Regaining composure, Karl said, "Marlo, I have never felt this way before. I know I just want to be with you for the rest of my life. I want to marry you." He drew her very close and enfolded her in his arms.

There was a strange mixture of warmth pulsating through her body and embarrassment about expressing her tender feelings. By nature, Marlo was not inclined to articulate affectionate emotions or use terms of endearment. "I want that too, Karl, very much," she said, her words nearly muffled in his chest. "I would be willing to move to East Germany."

Karl was quiet for a moment, calculating with care what he felt he needed to say. "Ah, Marlo, that's out of the question. There is no future here for an American wife and to pursue any kind of career. Once you become an East German citizen, you will not be permitted to travel to America even for the purpose of visiting your family. Besides, I would not want our children to grow up under a Communist regime as I've been forced to do. You know, before I met you, I almost decided to forget about going to the West and try to live as best I can in the GDR, even with all of its limitations. Marlo, now *I know* that leaving this country is the only solution for our future together."

"You mean *escape?*"

"Yes."

"Isn't that dangerous?"

"Well, there is a risk of getting caught and going to jail. But if I'm careful—*very* careful—I can do it."

"But what about your family? Won't you be isolated from them? How will they feel about that?"

"I'm not sure. I remember that before the wall went up, my father was serious about leaving East Germany. I think my leaving would be hard on my mother. Maybe sometime in the future, we could get them out of the country. In the meantime, they will have Albert for emotional support and assistance."

"Are you sure, *absolutely sure*, you want to do this?"

"Of course."

"When?"

"I've been thinking about that ever since I got your telegram. Next summer. Then we can meet and study together next fall at Tübingen. I hear that's a good university with a reputable medical school."

"That's a wonderful idea!" Marlo wrapped her arms around Karl's waist, pulled him tightly close to her, and buried her face in his chest.

They returned to the center of Dresden and continued their plans for the future as they promenaded around the city's large public park, Der Grosse Garten.

"Tomorrow I'll take the train with you to Plauen."

"Oh, Karl, how lovely! We'll have more time together."

"I think we'd better keep our future plans to ourselves. I don't want my mother to get nervous about our plans for marriage or my leaving the country. It will raise too many questions and problems."

Marlo nodded.

Bells rang out from the nearby Kreuzkirche. "That's an interesting church," exclaimed Karl. He and his family had attended services there occasionally. "Let's go to the special service. The children's choir will be singing. And there's the great Silbermann organ!" They went into the church and chose a pew near the back of the nave, where they could sit by themselves.

"This is a famous church restored to its original condition by contributions from all over the world," Karl whispered. "Former members of the children's choir, now living elsewhere in Europe and North America, were instrumental in promoting the project. You see, while they were on concert tours in other countries, some of their choir members went into hiding or sought political asylum. But they never lost their love for their homeland, for this church."

They sat there holding hands in church—something neither of them had ever done before in their lives. Marlo found the choral and organ music enchanting. It brought happy memories of her own musical endeavors and church experiences of her childhood. "What a wonderful way to bring to a close our time together," she said softly, her eyes wide with delight. "Thank you."

The following morning, Eva, Kurt, and Albert gave Marlo an affectionate send-off. As Karl and Marlo sped away from the family storefront, Marlo said, "Gee, I think your parents like me."

"I *know* they do." He leaned over from the wheel and playfully nibbled on Marlo's ear. On the way to the train station, Karl pulled his car into the police headquarters so Marlo could have the officer stamp an exit visa imprint in her passport.

They boarded the train and were fortunate to find a compartment to themselves. Providence seemed to have smiled upon them. The train developed engine trouble between Chemnitz and Plauen. They had extra time together.

Upon arriving in Plauen, Marlo noticed she was not filled with the heaviness of sorrow she had felt in Berlin when she and Karl had to say farewell. Rather, she was filled with great joy over finding a man she could love and respect, someone who returned that love and respect in full measure. She was on an emotional high, knowing she would see Karl again in a few months.

"I'll be returning to California in two weeks. Let's write to each other often. I'm not the best letter writer in the world. It takes me so long to get a letter finished once I've begun! But I'll try to write once a week."

"How do you say it in English . . . Ah, okay!" They laughed.

"Do be careful leaving for the West, Karl!"

"I will. I love you, Marlo Farrell."

"And I love you, Karl Mann." They embraced and kissed passionately.

Karl stood on the platform and waved to Marlo until the train was out of sight. Sullen, he sat down to await a train heading back home.

CHAPTER 14

Two weeks later, Marlo was back on the university campus in Stockton, California. She had only one semester to complete before graduation. She had heard from Karl that he had returned to his studies at Humboldt University in East Berlin. Through their correspondence, each had confessed to the other their difficulty keeping focused on class assignments. They lived from week to week on the letters flowing from one continent to the other. It was like bread for a malnourished soul! The letters kept their hopes alive and their dreams for the future vivid.

Marlo was shocked to find that for the first time in her academic journey, she had received a C on an essay test in her course on European fourteenth-through-sixteenth centuries Renaissance in literature and art. She was good at crafting essays. She thought she knew her subject. But it seemed to be symptomatic of the distraction of romance. *Focus focus focus!* Bringing both fists down hard on her dormitory room desk, she uttered an epithet that had never before crossed her lips: "Damn!" She laughed at herself. "Why didn't I say the word my sister Janice always used, *reservoir?* Yes, *oh reservoir!*" She knew she would have to work very hard to retain an A for the course at the end of the semester. She did.

When Marlo turned twenty-one in March, she was surprised by a delivery to her room in the dormitory. There was a knock at the door. Marlo stepped up to the door and opened it. Standing before her was a young man wearing a delivery uniform. "I have a delivery for a Ms. Marlo Farrell."

"That's me!"

It was an arrangement of twenty-one red roses. She opened the card. It was from Karl. He had asked a friend in West Berlin to send the roses to her by Fleurop.

A little package also arrived in the mail from Karl. It was a beautiful diamond engagement ring. Karl had sold his bicycle in order to help pay for the ring.

Marlo was overwhelmed by these gifts. Tears flowed.

Having accelerated her studies with an unusually high number of semester credits, she was graduated from UOP Raymond College in June of 1968 with a master's degree. She returned to her parents' home now in Santa Rosa, California. Her family had since moved from Bakersfield when her father was appointed a district superintendent of forty-six churches and their pastors in a sector of northern California.

Marlo's plan was to live with her parents and her little sister, Diane, to wait for Karl's escape from the GDR. She anxiously awaited word. Every evening, she was transfixed before the televised nightly news coverage of unrest in Eastern Europe and the Balkan States. People of her generation were in revolt. Political pundits echoed the conjectures of the US State Department that there seemed to be a growing fracture in the Soviet bloc.

"Oh my goodness!" Marlo murmured. "How much more insufferable despotism can this weary world endure?" In the wake of such tragedies as the assassinations of President Kennedy and Martin Luther King Jr. and the persisting bloodbath in Vietnam, Marlo saw upheaval as ubiquitous. Though by nature not an activist in public arenas, she still cherished the peace movement and supported the work of Amnesty International, which shone the spotlight on egregious persecution and imprisonment of innocent people where tyrants ruled with unabashed mendacity.

She thought it ironic that such peace-loving East German people like the Mann household were citizens of a Communist government supporting North Vietnam in that Asian conflict. Then Marlo's thoughts turned to Karl. *How will this unrest in Eastern Europe affect Karl's chances of leaving the GDR?* she mused.

CHAPTER 15

Political tensions were heightening in East Germany in late spring of 1968 particularly over the government's role in the Vietnam War. Partisan arguments raged on the radio. In addition, behind the Iron Curtain were restless people rebelling against long-suffered oppression perpetrated by beguiling dictators with no lack of hubris.

Through the summer months, the situation was no less evident among the college student generation in Czechoslovakia. Many of them, like their Western counterparts, adopted the method of organized public demonstrations. There was a hunger for social and economic reforms. Youth in the GDR were displaying similar attitudes.

Karl observed what was going on. A part of him watched with quiet delight. Another part of him was infused with angst. His university classes were to conclude at the end of June. He knew he and Fritz would have to make their move soon after school was out. *But when exactly?*

With only a week of school remaining, the two men were walking to their dormitory after class one afternoon. "You know, Karl, I think we ought to take advantage of the current unrest and leave the GDR now."

"But Fritz, the borders may be under greater surveillance than anything we've known before."

"Yes, I know all that, but I'm concerned that the longer we wait, the more difficult it will be to get across the border. It seems like there is going to be a gradual military buildup, especially to the south. I really believe this is the time to make our move. If we don't, we may lose our chances forever! Remember how it was with your parents and mine? They waited too long to make their move into West Berlin. Then the wall went up."

"True, true. Why don't we spend some time this weekend making some final plans?"

Saturday found Fritz and Karl sitting on the grass in a public park to discuss their plans rather than risk having their conversation overheard by progovernment informants.

"I think our best opportunity is to get into Czechoslovakia and from there to Austria," proposed Karl.

"Right. But I doubt if our government will issue visas to Czechoslovakia right now. Trouble seems to be brewing there."

"You may be right."

"I have another idea. Maybe we can get visas for Hungary. Why don't we enter Hungary? Then we can slip over the Hungarian-Yugoslav border. My family has friends living near the border in the Hungarian town of Nagykanizsa."

"Do you think they would try to help us get over the border?"

"I don't know for sure, but it's certainly worth a try."

"So from Hungary, we can either go into Yugoslavia or Austria, or from Czechoslovakia into Austria, depending upon what we're up against. The more options the better, eh?"

Fritz nodded. "I'll write to our family friends in Nagykanizsa and ask them to send us an official invitation so we can obtain a visitor's visa. You know, that town near the border isn't a normal tourist stop, so we are really dependent upon an invitation from these people in order to get into the country."

"Agreed," said Karl.

Fritz sent that all-important letter in the mail that very day. Three weeks had come and gone before an answer came. The invitation for a brief visit was issued. The men applied for the visitor's visa to Hungary. They waited for what seemed like an eternity for the government's reply. Ten days later they got their notification: visa application *accepted!* It was now the end of July.

Karl now had the difficult task of informing the family of his plan to leave the country. To his surprise, his mother and father were supportive. "My son, in the West you'll have a better future in medicine . . . and a better life with Marlo," assured Eva though tearfully.

"Unless things change dramatically for the better here, we'll find a way to join you at a later date," asserted his father.

Albert gave his brother a thumbs-up.

They all embraced.

It took another two weeks to surreptitiously gather his medical textbooks, school documents, and pack personal belongings. It was not easy stuffing everything into one small suitcase. In his imagination, it seemed as though GDR secret police were lurking wherever he went. He and Fritz needed to meet again to make final plans for their departure. Karl sent a letter to Marlo stating he and Fritz were about to leave for Hungary and within another week or so—around mid-August—she would hear from him in free Austria. He was elated. Karl looked in a mirror and smiled at himself.

CHAPTER 16

The rhythmic chug of the locomotive carried its human cargo along the countryside toward the destination of Budapest. Getting on the train at Dresden had been routine and uncomplicated. It was a balmy August evening when the pair disembarked at the city's main depot in Pest. Moving haltingly through unfamiliar surroundings, the two looked like tourists. From Pest, they gazed beyond the Danube to the lights beginning to shine across the hills of Buda. They appeared like sparkling jewels.

Karl and Fritz wandered through the center of Pest and slipped into Kis Kakuk for supper—a typical Hungarian inn featuring gypsy music. They spent the night at the modest Hotel Express, a youth hostel on Beethoven Street.

Sunday morning, cathedral bells pealed, arousing the youthful refugees from their slumber. The hostel was buzzing with activity. Many European and North American students were on holiday, occupying every available bed at Hotel Express. Karl and Fritz lost no time showering, shaving, and getting to the cafeteria quickly before the best food selections would be gone. They succeeded.

Karl pulled from his coat pocket a picture postcard of Budapest that he had purchased at a train station kiosk. He addressed it to Marlo and simply wrote the cryptic message "First stop on the way. Love, Karl" and dated it.

After breakfast, they boarded a bus heading southwest to Nagykanizsa. The 190-kilometer journey passed by the extraordinary seventy-five-kilometer-long Balaton Lake. Camping spots were deserted, awaiting the onslaught of campers at the more favorable time of late August and early September. Avid camper that he was, Karl was quite impressed with the scenic beauty. A multilane highway extended only as far as Siófok, at lakeside, about halfway to Nagykanizsa. Slow two-lane traffic and frequent bus stops along the way lengthened the journey beyond expectation, making Karl restless. By midafternoon, they were at their destination—only twenty kilometers from the Yugoslav border. Both men felt a surge of excitement but also of apprehension. Maybe their anxiety was an intuitive nudge that they were being studied very carefully by a figure hidden in the shadows. German tourists in a remote border town like this were suspect.

Fritz found their way to a familiar modest clapboard house with faded, peeling blue paint. A knock brought Bo Renkach to the door.

"Hello! Fritz, is that you?"

"Yes! Hello!"

"Well, it has been a long time, my boy! Come in, come in."

Bo reached out for an embrace. They slapped each other on the back as they gripped one another.

"This is Karl Mann, about whom I wrote in the letter."

"I am very pleased to meet you, Mr. Mann."

"And I am happy to meet you, Mr. Renkach."

They joined hands in a hearty greeting.

"Please, sit down. Can I get you anything? Coffee or tea perhaps?"

"Nothing for me, thank you," Karl responded.

"I'm fine. Thank you very much," said Fritz.

Karl looked about at the rustic dark wood paneling, antique furniture, and knickknacks that adorned the rather small living room.

"You have a very nice home. It feels warm and cozy," Karl said.

"Thank you. Have you boys had a good trip so far?"

"Yes," replied Fritz.

"You certainly have a beautiful lake in the area. We passed it on the road from Budapest," commented Karl.

Bo Renkach nodded in agreement. "Excellent fishing there."

They sat through a moment of awkward silence. Bo cleared his throat. "We were happy to get your letter and extend to you our invitation to come here, but frankly, we were surprised you would think to come this way for a holiday. Young people like to go to the city night clubs for the music, dancing, and drinking, don't you?" Bo's eyebrows flew up.

Fritz darted a glance at Karl, who gave a slight shrug. "Oh," stated Fritz with a nervous laugh under his breath, "I suppose so." Quickly changing the subject, he asked, "Is Mrs. Renkach at home?"

"She has gone to the market, should be back soon. Are you sure you don't want anything after such a long ride? Pilsner, mineral water, coffee, tea?"

"I'll have some mineral water, thank you," replied Fritz.

"I'll have the same, thank you," Karl said.

Bo went to the kitchen and asked with a raised voice, "Well, how are your parents, Fritz?"

"Oh, just fine. They asked me to tell you folks hello."

Karl stepped over to a window and peered out through the curtain. Again he sensed a sleuth-like gaze coming from somewhere out there. He looked back at Fritz, cocked his head, shrugged his shoulders, and rolled his eyes.

Bo returned from the kitchen with bottled water. "I have not seen your parents in years, and our correspondence is not so good. When last together, your father's business was doing very well indeed. How is it now?"

"Not so good, I'm sorry to say."

"Oh? Hmm."

"Well, you see, the government does not think my father should own both the furniture factory and the retail store. They are ordering him to relinquish one or the other to government control. The state seems most interested in acquiring the factory. Of course, they will pay him for it, but probably not what it is really worth."

"My, my! How does your father feel about that?"

"Not so good, as you might imagine. He has spent his whole life developing and expanding his business. I'm afraid this whole thing is taking a toll on his health."

"Has the government made an offer on the factory?"

"One hundred thousand marks."

Bo Renkach shook his head in disbelief. "Oh, the factory is certainly worth much more than that!"

There was silence. The men sipped their mineral water.

"It sounds like life is hard in the GDR," Bo offered.

Karl replied, "It doesn't seem to be getting any better. We have friends near Meissen who farm. The government has been expanding its farming cooperative program over the past ten years, and these folks have to give up most of their acreage to the cooperative. The system does not seem to be working as well as the authorities boasted it would."

"What kind of work does your father do, Karl?"

"He owns a grocery store in Meissen. It's been in the family for a long time. Business is good, but it is hard to procure quality merchandise in Eastern Europe. For example, the Soviet Union limits the supply of over-the-counter and prescription medicines. And it is very hard to obtain superior commodities from the West."

Bo shook his head in silence. "For many years, Fritz's father and I used to do a lot of business together. I had a large furniture store in Budapest and ordered regularly from his factory."

At that moment, Rosa Renkach came through the door with a bulging shopping bag. "Ah, Fritz! Welcome!" She put down the bag and hugged him.

"It is so good to see you again, Mrs. Renkach."

"And you must be Karl Mann," she said with a warm smile.

Karl acknowledged her gesture. They shook hands.

"Welcome to our home. Are you boys hungry? I should get supper started."

Rosa busied herself in the kitchen, preparing special Hungarian cuisine, while Bo showed the fellows through the house. He offered an in-depth commentary on the various curios and antiques he and his wife had accumulated over the years. Most of the furniture had come from his Budapest store and were crafted by Fritz's father. They were never able to have children, so they collected knickknacks, and each had its own unique personality.

"Well, tell us about your holiday. Are you planning to be in Hungary long?" inquired Rosa during the meal.

Karl and Fritz sat stiffly, looking at each other with the realization that they had not discussed how they would broach the subject of their escape plans. Karl tilted his chin toward Fritz and looked down at his plate of food. Fritz got the message.

"Well," Fritz began, laboring to find the right words, "Karl and I have found life in the GDR intolerable. The government is—there's no other way to say it—*pernicious*."

Bo and Rosa slowly lowered their utensils and stared at each other with speechless astonishment.

"I must be direct with you," continued Fritz. "There is no other way to say it. We are really on more than a holiday. We are—"

"You mean to say," interrupted Bo, "that you are leaving your families as well as your country?"

"That's correct," added Karl. "Actually, our families have given us their moral support, their blessings."

"Things must be pretty bad for you to take such drastic steps and jeopardize your medical careers," Rosa said.

"It's just the way we happen to feel. We can't speak for anyone else," said Fritz. "Besides, Karl has a personal reason for wanting to leave."

"Last fall I met an American student in Berlin," Karl explained. "We fell in love, and we want to get married. I don't see a good future for her in the GDR. She has a good mind. She wants to teach. She would have difficulty obtaining a teaching credential in East Germany. Given her religious affections and political philosophy, not to mention her American citizenship, I suppose you could say that her chances are probably nil. She is close to her family, but there's no guarantee she would be allowed to leave the country to visit them in the United States. I believe that would put a strain on our marriage." Karl paused for a moment for a drink of mineral water and to study the countenance of Bo and Rosa. "To be honest with you, I am feeling somewhat suffocated by the degree of government intrusion into our personal lives and the coercive methods employed to get you to join the Communist Party."

"Of course, no system of government anywhere is ideal," asserted Rosa.

"I understand what you are saying," Karl replied, "but from what I have learned about life in the West, there is something better—though not perfect, as you say—than what we are experiencing."

"I admire your courage, both of you," said Bo. "What are your plans now?"

"Well, Mr. Renkach," replied Fritz, "is it possible for you folks to help us find a way across the border into Yugoslavia or Austria?"

"I really don't know, Fritz," Bo replied nervously, wringing his hands. "You know, problems are developing in Czechoslovakia. Students have been demonstrating in Prague for many months. There are strong winds of change blowing across Eastern Europe . . ."

"And around our country, people are very tense, scared, not knowing what will happen," Rosa interjected.

"Yes, we've been following the news," said Fritz.

"It appears Alexander Dubček may be in trouble with the Kremlin," said Bo. "There's talk that the Soviet Union may soon send Warsaw Pact troops into Czechoslovakia to temper, if not crush, Dubček's social and economic reforms that have growing popularity with the people there."

"We think the border patrol may be enlarged along the Austrian border due to Soviet pressure on our government," Rosa stated.

"Then do you think we would have better luck crossing into Yugoslavia?" pressed Fritz.

"I don't know what to say about that, Fritz. Some folks in town have been saying there are plainclothes police looking for refugees. They are like bounty hunters. If they find a refugee from an Eastern European country, they'll turn 'em in for a good sum of money. If a Hungarian gets caught aiding and abetting a refugee, he can get into serious trouble with the authorities."

Neither Fritz nor Karl said anything for a few minutes. They glanced at each other intermittently, sensing the shared thought of not endangering Bo and Rosa. It was clear to them that the Renkaches were uncomfortable discussing the matter.

Finally, Karl broke the silence. "Thank you for the warning. We will be cautious. We don't want to cause you any difficulties."

Fritz concurred adamantly.

Bo gave a sweeping gesture with his hands as if to wave the issue aside as inconsequential. But his wife looked measurably relieved.

"I think it would be well for us to leave here in the morning," Fritz suggested.

"Please don't feel you must rush away on our account," their hostess said. "We are happy to have you stay longer."

"Thank you for your kindness, Mrs. Renkach, really, but we should leave tomorrow."

Monday morning, August 19, was warm and humid with thunderclouds forming over nearby hills.

"It doesn't look like a very good day for traveling, boys," counseled Mrs. Renkach. "Are you sure you wouldn't rather stay another day?"

"Yes, we are sure," replied Fritz, "but thank you anyway."

"We do appreciate your hospitality," said Karl.

"We were happy to have you with us," said Bo. "It's been good seeing you again, Fritz. Which way will you go from here?"

"I think we will follow highway E96 to the Yugoslav border."

Rosa gave the boys a sack of food for their journey. "Do be careful, and good luck!" exclaimed the Renkaches as they gave both boys a hug.

The young men headed into town on foot, oblivious to an interested third party lingering behind in an automobile. But Karl began to have a vague sense of an ominous presence. Thunderheads were still forming from horizon to horizon.

They arrived at the bus depot, only to receive the disappointing news that the transnational bus had just pulled out of the station for Zagreb, Yugoslavia. Another bus bound for that country would not be along for several hours. They decided to begin walking. After all, the distance to the border wasn't too great.

No sooner did they get to the edge of town on their way to the main highway than a car pulled alongside of them. "I am going to Yugoslavia," shouted the driver in broken German. "Do you want a ride?"

The stranger's solicitude made them hesitant. Karl felt downright suspicious. "How did he know to speak to us in German?" Karl whispered to Fritz.

"Your offer is kind, but no thank you," replied Karl, pretending to struggle with a false *broken* German. "We are visiting friends." The driver seemed satisfied and drove on out of sight.

"Do you think that was a secret policeman? asked Karl.

"Or maybe a bounty hunter, eh?"

"I think we're too conspicuous here. Maybe we need to go in another direction."

"Yeah. Maybe we should return to Budapest," proposed Fritz.

"It's a difficult choice. We've come so far! You can almost see Yugoslavia over those hills," Karl said with a tone of resignation.

They stood motionless for a moment, staring at the ground and then staring at each other. Almost imperceptibly, smiles formed upon their faces simultaneously. Slapping each other on the back, they made their way back to the bus terminal.

Their climb aboard the bus for Budapest was well-timed. A torrential thunderstorm broke loose, pelting the landscape mercilessly. During the ride, they enjoyed the food Mrs. Renkach had prepared. By the time they arrived in Budapest, the storm had ceased. They hastened to the train station and booked passage for Prague, but they really intended to get off at Bratislava. That town was so close to the Austrian border. Karl and

Fritz barely had time to grab a quick snack at an espresso shop before departure.

They settled into their train car compartment. Perhaps it was wishful thinking or simply lending credence to aborting their original plan that led Karl to wonder, *Maybe the political upheaval in Czechoslovakia will provide a good cover for us. After all, what East German in his right mind would dare to attempt an escape to the West at a time of heightened tension?*

When the train stopped at the border near Bratislava, Karl and Fritz noticed an unusually large number of border guards—all Czech soldiers, who routinely checked their passports and visas. The soldiers seemed to be laughing and joking among themselves as they moved through the coach.

Despite the friendliness of the guards, the military buildup at the border discouraged Fritz and Karl from leaving the train. The risk seemed too great. They decided to wait and try another spot farther up the line yet still close to the Austrian border. If necessary, they would go all the way to Prague and make further plans from there.

Fritz and Karl breathed a sigh of relief as the last guard disembarked and the train jerked forward. Karl was impressed with the southern landscape of the country, which he had never seen before. The wooded Carpathian Mountains were particularly awesome.

As the train moved farther northwest, they noticed a large compound congested with military armored equipment and cargo under heavy guard.

Karl turned to Fritz. "I am thinking there is something more than a practice military maneuver being staged."

Fritz nodded. "Remember what Bo Renkach said about the Russians' displeasure with Dubček."

It was late that Monday night when the train pulled into the Prague station. The atmosphere of the city was charged with gaiety—not quite what the two young Germans expected, but a welcome relief nonetheless. They decided to walk to the university and found a hospitable place for the night at the Christian Student Center. They were happily surprised to find a group of students there from Stuttgart. Karl and Fritz discussed their plans into the early morning hours.

"We would like to help you come to West Germany," they assured the two. "But it is impossible for us to do anything."

"We understand," replied Karl, "but we really appreciate your support."

"Why don't you go to the West German Mission office tomorrow and see what they can do for you?" one of the students suggested.

Karl and Fritz agreed. With that settled, they all went to sleep.

It was almost ten o'clock when they awoke on Tuesday morning. The previous day's events had proven to be strenuous. They enjoyed brunch at the Espresso Kajetanka under the battlement of the castle with an exquisite vista. They took a stroll along the Vltava River with its unique array of boatels. Their conversation was light and reflective of their new experiences. They recalled previous visits to this great city of a thousand spires. Karl, especially, liked Prague. The old section of the city situated high on a bluff was particularly charming and historic.

They discovered that the Mission of the Federal Republic of Germany was not scheduled to open until two o'clock, following a typically long lunch break. They walked briskly through the park and chuckled to see a cat sparring with the remnant of a billboard poster announcing the Prague Spring Festival now history, buffeted by the wind. Across the park in front of the mission were a few young people—perhaps students—milling around the entrance while armed sentries stood nearby with watchful glances. Fritz and Karl began to feel apprehensive, but they mustered enough courage to mount the steps of the rather plain office building and disappear through the entrance door.

After a wait of nearly an hour, having tendered their passports for inspection, Fritz Schimmel and Karl Mann were escorted by the receptionist into a small office of a junior diplomat. He was a short, stout middle-aged man with a friendly round ruddy face accentuated by a finely groomed handlebar mustache meticulously waxed and curled. His deep-blue eyes were nearly hidden under bushy eyebrows. He gestured for the two to be seated.

"So you want to leave the GDR for the West too!"

"Too?" they exclaimed in unison.

"Lately we've had many of you—mostly students—coming here for help."

"That's why we are here," Fritz said matter-of-factly.

"Mr. Schimmel, Mr. Mann, we do admire your resolve, your boldness." The administrator got up from his chair and walked over to a window behind his desk. Parting the sheer lace curtains, he looked out upon the street scene. He jerked his head in the direction of his glance. "Do you see what's going on out there, what's happening in Prague?" He turned to look at his guests.

They nodded without a word.

"Under conditions of relative normalcy, it would be difficult to grant your request, gentlemen." He looked once again out the window. "But now, with things . . . shall we say . . . precarious, it is impossible . . . *impossible*. The situation is sensitive, tense. One false move and our tenuous position here will be severely compromised."

Karl and Fritz were obviously crestfallen.

"I know how disappointing this must be to you. I am sorry . . . *truly sorry*."

"Do you have any suggestions as to what we might do now?" Karl asked.

With a kind of learned diplomatic caution, the officer replied with measured words, "No, I am sorry, there is nothing we can do, no suggestions to offer."

"I see," Karl muttered with resignation. "Well, thank you for your time."

"Not at all, gentlemen. Here are your passports. Enjoy your stay in Prague. Good day and good luck."

They shuffled down the steps at the entrance. Karl stopped abruptly, seemingly lost in deep thought while Fritz walked on ahead. "Hey, Fritz! Let's try the American embassy!"

"Why not! We have nothing to lose."

Again they surrendered their passports and waited in the lobby of the US embassy for a long time. Finally, emerging from an office down the corridor and approaching them was a tall, slender silver-haired gentleman dressed in a finely tailored dark-blue pinstripe suit. He greeted them with a warm smile and firm handshake.

In his halting German, he said, "Boys, it is such a beautiful afternoon! Let us go into the garden for our visit."

Fritz and Karl followed him into spacious grounds forming a quadrangle within the embassy complex. A variety of shrubs and flowers softened the sharp angular walls. The three men gathered next to an ornamental tree that might otherwise serve as a subject of conversation.

"I think we can speak more freely here," said the man as he made gestures as if to point out certain features of the tree.

"We'll get right to the point, sir," Fritz began. "We want to leave the German Democratic Republic. We want your help—we *need* your help."

The diplomat looked down and bit his lip, rubbing his forehead vigorously. "Frankly, our government would like to help you, but—"

"It's the political situation right now, is that it?" Fritz interrupted.

"I'm afraid that's right. Some we have tried to help have gotten caught. Under international treaty agreements, the refugees are returned to their homelands for prosecution . . . and likely prison sentence."

"We have tried the West German Mission without success. You have given us essentially the same story," Karl contended with a tone of irritation. "What do you suggest we do?"

"Please believe me when I say I can understand how you must feel . . . Well, maybe I can't. But I *know* you are extremely disappointed, frustrated. So am I! The only thing I can suggest is that you try in your own way to get across the border to Austria. There is one thing in your favor. The border is patrolled by Czechs. They just might let you slip through as long as you don't try to pass through the main road checkpoint."

"Why not across the Czech—West German border?" quizzed Karl.

"Because there is quite a heavy military buildup in that region. The latest intelligence information we're getting indicates Warsaw Pact troops are moving this way. We suspect something is going to happen soon in this area. So I think you'd be better off trying the border frontier south of Ceske Budejovice or Znojmo. And I wouldn't waste any time getting started."

"Thank you," said Fritz. Karl nodded in agreement.

"One more thing you should know. The border fence is electrified. And as far as we know, there are no antipersonnel mines planted near the fence. Please do not quote me on anything I have told you. Perhaps I've told you more than I should. Our policy is one of denial if we are quoted on sensitive issues." He returned their documents to them and led them back into the building. Walking them to the entrance, he took their hands and earnestly wished them the best of luck.

It was late in the afternoon when Karl and Fritz conferred with their student friends at the Christian Student Center. A good deal of support developed for the idea of trying to escape through the frontier fence. One of the Stuttgart students, who spoke Slovak fluently, volunteered to go to the store and buy a pair of wire-cutters and safety gloves for Karl and Fritz.

"Later tonight, we're leaving for Vienna. Why don't you ride with us as far as the border?" offered another student from Stuttgart. "We can find an isolated spot to let you out."

"We'll be delighted!" replied Karl. "I've always wanted to walk through the Vienna Woods!"

Karl posted a card to Marlo with cryptic details. By nine o'clock, the carload of students was en route to Vienna. It was nearly 11:00 PM as the August 20 sun had set, casting lengthening shadows of dusk. The car pulled into a rest area beside the highway in a mountainous area a few kilometers north of the Czech-Austrian border.

"Well, this is where we part," said the student behind the wheel.

"Wish we could take you the rest of the way," said another.

"Ah, you've done a lot for us, and we're grateful," replied Fritz.

"Maybe our paths will cross again in West Germany, *soon!*" exclaimed Karl. The close proximity of the border to freedom heightened his expectations. In his own psyche, he believed that freedom was now a fait accompli. He felt he and Fritz had traveled such a distance and overcome so many obstacles. Getting beyond the fence was now a mere formality.

"We wish you well! Our prayers go with you. God bless you!" rang the chorus of cheers from the students.

"And God be with you for safe travel!" shouted Fritz.

They stood silently and watched as the car sped away, winding around a curve and vanishing from sight. It was very quiet. Not even a bird's chirping or cricket sounds were heard. Karl and Fritz were spellbound by the peculiar stillness all around them. Then the far-off sound of a diesel truck laboring up the grade shook them out of their reverie.

"We'd better cross the road and disappear into the woods, quick!" insisted Karl.

They slipped into the forest with its dense undergrowth. A very faint glow on the western horizon helped them chart their course southward. They continued to push through the thicket and trees downhill. Then they approached a meadow.

"Look, Fritz! Does that look like a fence beyond that row of trees?"

"Can't quite make it out."

"Maybe a hundred meters."

"Karl, let's lie low here until it gets a little darker."

"Good idea."

Not far behind them were sounds of many vehicles as if in a convoy, grinding their gears. They seemed to be heading toward the border crossing a short distance away. *Uh-oh!* Karl thought to himself. He and Fritz hugged the earth in the tall grass at the meadow's edge, waiting for darkness to bring its gift of camouflage.

CHAPTER 17

It was late afternoon of August 20 in Santa Rosa, California. Marlo was looking through a stack of wedding magazines. Tears began to well up in her eyes as she thought, *I never imagined I would ever get married. I wasn't interested in guys.*

She remembered how she had participated in weddings of her older sisters. When Doreen got married to Dick Heath, Marlo was thrilled when she was asked to be the flower girl.

"She was just six years old," recalled Doreen. "She wore a pink dress and scattered flower petals in front of me. Oh, how excited she was about being a flower girl!"

A few years later in 1955 came the wedding of Janice and John Emory. It was their wish for Marlo to be an acolyte. *Wow! I was able to light all the candles on two large candelabra*, she recalled to herself.

When Linda got married to Lee Muncie, Marlo was elevated to the role of junior bridesmaid at age thirteen. *I was the first to walk down the staircase and the aisle.*

"She did it with poise," remembered Linda.

Marlo's thoughts went back to the kiss at the Meissen train station and, later, the day Karl proposed to her at Pillnitz. Though it was not the first time a boy had kissed her, it was the first time she liked it. *This is the one, and no other,* Marlo had thought at the time. It gave her goose bumps just thinking about it.

"Marlo!" her father called out. "I think you'll want to see this news report on TV."

She ran into the living room, where her parents and her little sister, Diane, were seated.

Marlo's heartbeat began to race as she watched the story unfold about what was happening at that moment in Eastern Europe.

"At 11:00 PM Central European time," the news commentator reported, "Warsaw Pact troops stormed into Czechoslovakia to put down the Dubček government. An estimated one hundred thousand troops and over four thousand tanks swarmed into the ill-defended country, blocking all border-crossing points. The whereabouts of Alexander Dubček is unknown at this hour. The US Central Intelligence Agency speculates that Soviet authorities may have captured him . . ."

The television audio began to fade from Marlo's attention as she started to wonder how this development might be impacting Karl. Visual images on the screen became a blur.

Marlo's father reached out to console her. "Let's not jump to any conclusions about Karl," he said calmly. "I'm sure you'll hear from him soon."

Marlo, her parents, and Diane looked at one another incredulously.

CHAPTER 18

A breeze wafted across the meadow, causing the tall grass to wave lazily in the dim light at the Czech frontier. Soon the mantel of darkness spread over the landscape like a comforter.

Fritz gave Karl a poke with his elbow. "I think it's okay to move out now," he whispered.

"Right! Let's go." A wavering tone of anxiety caught in Karl's throat.

As they walked cautiously through the tall grass, they could barely see an outline of a stand of trees and the fence line in the distance. Karl's breathing was shallow though his heart was pounding fiercely. When they got within ten meters of the fence, the ground cover came to an abrupt end. The authorities provided an open lane on both sides of the fence, endlessly it seemed, through the countryside. There were no signs of lookout towers. There was no evidence of sentries patrolling on foot or in vehicles up and down the buffer zone. There were no floodlights within view. The area around them was dark.

They slowly advanced to the fence. Karl and Fritz slipped on their gloves and took the wire-cutters from their pockets. Each snip of wire caused them to wince as the sound seemed to them to be amplified enough to echo throughout the little valley, just as surely as their throbbing hearts might well be heard by border guards at the road three kilometers away. Finally, a square section of wiring had been cut away sufficient for them to squirm through on their bellies.

Would cutting the electrified fence break the circuit and sound an alarm? Karl wondered. He couldn't hear anything. But the thought of that possibility prompted him to move swiftly into the wooded area with Fritz following on his heels. With only a sliver of moonlight, the going was slow.

Karl stopped and took Fritz's arm. "Think of it, Fritz! We're on free Austrian soil!"

"Ha! Tomorrow morning, Vienna!"

"We did it! We did it! Fritz, we are free!"

They spontaneously set their feet upon an impromptu jig. The forest was their dance hall. Strauss could not have been more pleased especially if the fellows would prefer to dance a waltz.

"Fritz, I suppose we'd better find a place to bed down for the night. At dawn we can find the road and hitch a ride to Vienna."

They walked a few meters farther and then froze in their tracks, absolutely stood fast, paralyzed.

"Karl, what's that ahead?"

"It's a fence . . . **another** fence!"

"I don't understand."

"Fritz, we must still be on Czech soil. Austria must be on the other side of that fence!"

"Karl, do you still have your wire-cutters?"

"Ah, no. I left them at the other fence. I didn't think we'd need them anymore."

"Yeah, well, I left mine back there too. I'll go back and retrieve—"

"Fritz! Look over there to your right. What's that?"

"It looks . . . like . . . ah . . . mmm . . . I think it's a house or shack or something like that."

"It looks dark. Maybe it's deserted."

"I sure hope you're right, Karl."

As they came closer to the structure, barking of dogs were heard.

"Uh-oh! That must be a border frontier post! Let's break for the fence fast!" yelled Karl.

Suddenly from nowhere, dogs darted out toward them. They were on very long leashes.

Fritz and Karl ran in different directions, sensing the futility of trying to scale an electrified fence. Karl climbed up into a tree but could not pull one leg up fast enough. A dog clenched its teeth into the cuff of his trousers. A burst of brilliant light momentarily blinded him. Soldiers had shot off flares in order to locate the two figures dashing through the darkness of the forest. Within minutes, soldiers had the two men in custody and took them to a roadside border station.

"It is with some reluctance that we bring you here," confessed one of the apprehending soldiers. "But once we saw something suspicious out there, we had to act."

How ironic that they should be taken by such unenthusiastic captors. Karl and Fritz were pleasantly surprised by the Czech's congeniality. From the border station, Karl and his comrade were transported to a jail in the city of Znojmo only about ten kilometers from the border but almost one hundred kilometers from Vienna—from the wonderful Vienna Woods . . . from the music of Strauss and Mozart and Beethoven . . . from freedom . . . from a long-distance telephone call to Marlo.

It was a very old and dirty jail, but the Czech authorities were humane in their treatment of prisoners. Karl and Fritz were allowed to write letters to their parents. These letters were routed directly to the German Democratic Republic without having to be screened and censored by the East German Embassy in Prague. Karl was even allowed to write to Marlo, although he would discover much later that the correspondence never arrived at its United States destination. Karl's parents received his letter before the East German authorities even learned of the attempted escape. The two fellows were granted the luxury of sharing the same cell during their eight-day detention at Znojmo.

The police officers who questioned Karl seemed friendly and sympathetic. "We have to fulfill treaty obligations by returning refugees to the GDR," they said apologetically.

The two were taken to a jail in Prague, where they remained for six days while arrangements were made for their deportation to East Germany. They were put in a bus with a number of other GDR refugees. En route to the East German border town of Zinwald, the bus developed transmission trouble. *That's a good omen,* Karl thought. But another bus was dispatched, and the men were eventually delivered to the border unshackled.

They saw a road sign that read "Welcome to the German Democratic Republic." *Welcome, ha!* Karl thought. He and the others stepped off the bus to be greeted by a number of German soldiers brandishing machine guns.

"You will be shot immediately if you make any false moves," warned the commanding officer.

The refugees were marched to a nearby cluster of secret police, who handcuffed them and squeezed them into a small hot van—a dark dungeon on wheels—and whisked them off to East Berlin.

"Humph," grumbled Fritz. "Just like the Nazi gestapos in the movies!"

Karl nodded with a glazed look over his face. He was feeling the gnawing sensation of defeat.

Upon arrival at the high-level secret-service prison in East Berlin, Karl was permanently separated from his friend Fritz. Each was subjected to repeated intense interrogation by the secret police. Every would-be defector was suspected of being an enemy spy.

After the first week, during which time the authorities were displeased with the results of questioning Karl, a cell mate appeared. Karl's suspicions were aroused. *Probably a government plant.* Karl was careful about what he said. After a week, the suspected informant mysteriously disappeared. Karl found himself with another appointment with the inquisition.

Karl was led into a small room and sat down on a wooden chair next to a desk. A nearby window afforded him an opportunity to get a glimpse of the outside world. Yes, he was given fifteen minutes a day in an exercise yard, but the high walls surrounding the yard obstructed the view. All he could see was the sky. This second-story office offered a view to the west. *A room with a view, if you please.*

A tall, lean bald secret-service officer with an angular face entered the room and took his place behind the desk. He summarily leafed through a file folder presumably containing documents on Karl. The man laid the folder aside, folded his hands on the desktop, and gave Karl an icy stare.

"You know, Mr. Mann, you will have absolutely no future as a practicing physician in the German Democratic Republic unless you change your attitude. We are satisfied at this point that you are not a spy. We have investigated your background thoroughly. You seem to be a brilliant medical student. It is a shame to throw away such a promising career. Why would you ever want to leave this country, a country that has given you so much and can give you so much more?"

With a faint smile upon his countenance, Karl silently stared at the officer.

The officer slammed his hands down on the top of the desk to emphasize his point. Standing at his place and riveting his eyes down upon Karl, he continued, "I do not understand your generation, Mr. Mann! You are so impatient. Of course, we have not reached perfection. We are a young republic. But we need men of your caliber to build this great nation. Karl Mann, you had better think seriously about changing your attitude, your way of thinking." He sat down again.

At that point, Karl had some unspoken words. *Yes, change your attitude. And suppose you do change your thinking. The government might not trust your sincerity. Being released from prison to resume life in this country is like being moved into a larger prison.*

Karl's glance out the window focused on a Pan Am jet taking off from West Berlin's Tempelhof Airport.

"Mr. Mann, what do you think about that?"

"Ah . . . about what, sir?"

"What I have just said to you," snapped the officer.

"Hmm . . . I was just looking at the plane taking off."

The secret-service officer wheeled around in his swivel chair and caught a glimpse of it. "And?"

"I would like to be sitting in that plane."

The officer pivoted around to face Karl. With a growling tone of condescension, he said, "Mr. Mann, your impertinence does not serve you well! You'll soon be sitting in a transport van, which will take you to our facility in Dresden. That is in your home district, where you must stand trial for violation of the law. I trust you will give serious thought to what I have said to you."

Karl was escorted by guards to his solitary-confinement cell—a small cubicle with a solid metal door in which there was a slot for the passage of food and water, an opaque window offering only a hint of sunlight, a metal cot attached to one wall, a hole in the floor for toileting, and a vent hole in the ceiling for air—stale air at that. Three weeks in this cell seemed an eternity. The announced move to Dresden offered—in Karl's mind at least—the prospect of better accommodations. The move would bring him closer to home, closer to his family. Any news about the disposition of his case would have been a relief, but the news about going to Dresden cheered him. And of course, there was the good possibility of hearing some news about Marlo and how she was coping with this situation.

Karl paced his cell. His impatience was getting the best of him. *This whole episode is crazy! I got better treatment from the Czechs than in my own country. What's happening to me? I have not been an enemy of my country, only an enemy to oppressiveness and lies. Now I'm afraid I'm becoming bitter toward the GDR. Wouldn't* *the government be just as glad to let me go? I wonder how Fritz is getting along. What have they done with him? Will I see him again? This is intolerable! God, give me the strength to get through this! One day I will be free . . . I **shall** be free!*

With his eyes wide with rage, his jaw set, his neck extended, and every artery, ligament, and muscle in his neck bulging, he yelled, **"Do you hear me! One . . . day . . . I . . . shall . . . be . . . free!"** Karl slapped the open palms of his hands against the cell wall. It stung mightily and brought tears to his eyes. Emotionally exhausted, he slumped down onto his cot and drifted into a deep sleep.

Chapter 19

Marlo had received the two postcards from Karl, which gave her reason to be jubilant. But soon after, a letter arrived from Kurt and Eva Mann with the news of Karl's capture and incarceration. She was devastated.

"Oh, I need to return to Germany! I want to be close to Karl."

"I don't think that's wise, Marlo," her mother said. "You know it's dangerous over there right now. Besides, neither you nor we have the money to pay for such a trip."

Knowing how her father dabbled in international affairs and knew some prominent global leaders, Marlo had an idea.

"Daddy, isn't there something you can do to intercede on Karl's behalf?"

"My dear, I just don't know. I'll have to think about it."

"Well, you *do* know important people."

"Like I said, I'll give it some thought. Give me time, Marlo."

A few days later, the stack of mail delivered to the house included a solicitation from Amnesty International. Esther Farrell nearly threw it in the trash but hesitated. Something told her to open the envelope and read the enclosure. It was obviously a motivational letter for the recipient to make a contribution to the organization. The executive director wrote story after story of innocent persons put in political prisons in various troubled regions of the world and how their families did not know where they were. Amnesty personnel worked tirelessly to locate detainees and notify their families. Amnesty also worked to secure the release of the accused.

"Wesley, I think you need to look at this," she said, holding out the Amnesty International communiqué.

He read it with great interest.

"Do you know the executive director?" Esther asked.

"No, but I think I'll send him a letter detailing Karl's circumstance. Maybe Amnesty can add him to their list of causes."

That evening at dinner, Wesley disclosed his plan to Marlo. It gave her a sense of renewed hope. She even ate her peas without a fuss!

CHAPTER 20

Moving day had come and gone. Karl spent the first night in an underground cell in the prison atop a hill in Dresden. If any place held the potential for absolute demoralization, this dark, dismal setting was the place. The next morning, he was ushered to a cell on the ground floor.

His new accommodation was not much different from what he had left behind in East Berlin. Days lengthened into weeks while Karl awaited his trial. The long, unproductive hours in solitary seemed to him psychological warfare. He surmised they were out to break his spirit. Karl was determined to beat them at their monstrous game.

Each day began at six o'clock. Karl received a bowl of water with which to wash himself and brush his teeth. While the law provided that he get fifteen minutes in the exercise yard each day, sometimes he did not get it, and sometimes he was given only five minutes.

Karl spent the long days in his cell developing a ritual for coping with his narrowly circumscribed world: He repeated over and over things he had learned in medical school, such as details of the circulatory, nervous, and respiratory systems. He dreamed up escape plans and how his adversaries might counter them. To keep busy, he forced himself to read thoroughly and systematically the sophomoric Communist press and books allowed him. He washed his hands three times a day, and he exercised in his cell doing push-ups and sit-ups. Now and then, he would think of Marlo—her beauty, her tenderness, her warmth, the sweet smell of her skin, the fresh fragrance of her hair, and their plans to be married. At times, it was almost as if she were in the cell with him. Despite the joy of thinking about her, the dashed hope threw him into a dark depression. His insides churned and ached. He decided he could no longer afford the luxury of such memories. So Karl chose to put himself on a rigorous schedule, shrinking his world to the inside of that prison, the inside of his cell. He blocked from his mind altogether the outside world he had left.

The idea is for me to keep busy and maintain a daily ritual. Don't allow yourself to get psychologically beat. That's **their** *game. I* **refuse** *to play their game! I* **refuse** *to abide by their rules! I am in charge of my life. I am the ruler of my little kingdom here.*

Karl began to enjoy his solitude. For a change of pace, one day he decided to create chess pieces out of his daily ration of bread. Unfortunately, a guard discovered this, and thereafter, Karl's bread allotment was reduced.

"If that happens again," the guard warned, "you will not get any more bread."

Karl knew that was a vain threat. The law required that he receive bread each day. But he took the warning as a challenge. He made miniature chessmen out of the bread. Once he completed a set, he popped them into his mouth one by one with glee as if he were devouring his adversaries.

From the beginning, Karl learned that inmates, though kept in their cells all day (except for the few minutes in the exercise yard), were not allowed to lie down on their beds. It was a matter of either standing, pacing, or sitting on the hard-backed chair bolted to the frame of the bed.

"The bed is for sleeping *at night*, Mann," the guard shouted. **"Get up!"**

The only freedom Karl felt he possessed was in the expanse of his own mind. Yet even that realm of thought was a target for his adversaries. They tried to harness the mind through propaganda. Reading material consisted of an occasional edition of an East German newspaper and prison library books of "special educational value"—Communist literature, some of which was in novel form but of poor literary quality in Karl's opinion—dreadfully pedantic!

"May I have a Bible to read, please?" Karl had asked with all due naïveté when he was initially incarcerated.

"Oh yes, of course. We'll get you a Bible," came the polite reply.

Karl would wait in vain. That's the way it was with many requests. He learned not to get his hopes up.

One night, Karl's sleep was disturbed by a great deal of commotion throughout the prison. The next morning, an elderly man was brought to Karl's cell and hurriedly deposited there. Karl figured something unusual was going on because the man was still wearing his street clothes and had a little bundle of personal belongings under his arm.

The two men just sat and stared at each other for a few minutes.

"Hello! My name is Karl Mann."

Without changing his sullen expression, the old gentleman responded, "Yah. Hello."

"What's going on out there?"

"You haven't heard?"

"Heard what?"

"This prison is filling up with people who have been protesting the government's involvement in the invasion of Czechoslovakia."

Karl bit his lip, shaking his head in disgust.

"My two sons and daughter-in-law are somewhere in this prison too," the stranger said.

"Oh?"

"Yes, my oldest son and his wife were overheard at a public place criticizing the intervention of our troops. My younger son was caught writing a protest in graffiti on the wall of a shop."

The old man slowly pulled a long wrinkled handkerchief from his trouser pocket and wiped his nose and eyes.

"I suppose if they had not resisted and insulted the police," he continued, "there would have been no need for an arrest."

The man looked down into the open top of the sack he was holding. Karl focused on what he had not noticed before. He could see several green sprigs of something with delicately sculptured leaves barely showing over the top of the bag.

"Say, what do you have there?" asked Karl.

"Carrots." The man's face and voice remained expressionless.

"Carrots!"

"Yes."

"Ah, aren't you lucky the guards didn't take them away from you! In here I'd forgotten what a fresh vegetable looked like! You were shopping, eh?"

"No, I was just leaving my house and crossing the road to feed my rabbits when . . ." The old man couldn't go on. His mouth quivered. His throat tightened.

"So that's when they came and arrested you?"

The man simply nodded. "I wonder what will become of my rabbits! How will they get fed?"

Karl was silent, not knowing what to say. He reached out and gave a reassuring pat on the man's shoulder. The old man was a bit relieved. Karl moved from his cot and sat down next to the man on the edge of the other cot.

"Well, I suppose we shouldn't let these carrots go to waste," said Karl's new cell mate. He tilted the bag toward Karl, offering him some of the orange root. They sat there munching. Karl was savoring the sweet flavor. He felt like a small child receiving a piece of candy as a reward for having done a good deed. The two visited for several hours until a guard came to take the old man away. They bade each other farewell as if they had been friends for many years.

The taste of the carrots remained in Karl's mouth. He savored it as long as he could. Meals were nothing to write home about. Oh yes, there were three meals a day, but no imagination: bread, tea, and coffee . . . bread, tea, and coffee . . . bread, coffee, and tea. Sometimes potato or rice was added. The coffee was more like a nondescript broth—thick and gritty.

"Can you bring me some vitamins?" the astute would-be physician asked.

"Oh yes. We will bring you some vitamins," one guard replied with a smirk.

And as with the Bible, Karl waited in vain.

Almost like a ghastly invasion from another world, the day for his appearance in court was about to arrive on November 20—three months to the day of his entry into the Dresden prison. Two days beforehand, his defense attorney came to see him.

"Hello, Karl. I realize you don't know me, but I'm an acquaintance of your parents. They asked me to take your case, so I made myself available to the court. Luckily, I was selected. Ah, here, I have something for you from home."

The lawyer unwrapped a package, revealing some meat sandwiches and chocolates. With the secret-service officers standing nearby to monitor the meeting, Karl felt almost guilty taking these treasures of sheer luxury. He took them and immediately devoured them.

"Mmm . . . I forgot how meat and chocolate taste! Thank you!"

"Oh, Karl, pardon me for my poor manners. My name is Martin Braun."

They shook hands. Maintaining a circumspect image, especially in the presence of the secret police, Martin Braun said, "You need not thank me for the food. They are from your parents."

Karl's thoughts flashed back to earlier days and home cooking. He so enjoyed his mother's home-baked breads and homemade wursts that filled plump sandwiches. And every Saturday, after cleaning the store and washing windows, his father would let him and his brother pick out any stick of candy from the shelf.

He recalled the old man with the carrots. Karl had been blessed then too with something special to eat. *I'm not so bad off after all.* Karl wondered how the old man and his family were doing. He wondered if the rabbits really had been looked after by neighbors. *Ahhh . . . rabbits are so soft.* Why was Karl preoccupied with the softness of rabbits? He had not touched anything smooth and fine for such a long time. He had not touched anyone for a long time. Nobody had gently touched him. That lack of sensitive human contact had left Karl emotionally starved. *Does anyone really appreciate the importance of such things until being deprived of them? Softness, touching, carrots, meat, chocolates?* It was torturous just thinking about it. He drove these thoughts from his mind and concentrated once again on the present moment. This was his strategy for psychological survival.

"How goes it with you, Karl?"

"Umm, it's pretty lonely in isolation. But I'm all right."

"Do you have any questions?"

"Ah, I don't know. I guess I don't know what to ask. Well, it seems to be taking so long to deal with my case."

"Karl, I've studied the legal documents compiled by the prosecutor. They've been very thorough in their investigation. That takes time. The court docket is crowded."

"I must ask you frankly, Mr. Braun, just how interested are you in defending me, of giving me what I want?"

"I'm here as a courtesy to your family, Karl. I've known your parents for some years, though I've seen you and your brother . . . ah . . ."

"Albert."

"Yes, Albert. I've seen you two briefly only once or twice when you were quite young. But of course, I'm interested in giving you the best defense possible. Whether I can give you *what you want* . . . well, I don't know. You need to tell me what you want."

"Acquittal! I want to be allowed to leave the country."

Braun slumped back in his chair, looked at the indictment page, and slowly shook his head.

"Frankly, Karl, there is nothing I can do to grant your wish. You have been quoted as saying that you want to leave the GDR. I have handled similar cases. Believe me, I am not optimistic, and I don't want to give you false hope. The government is cracking down severely on those who leave the country illegally."

"You mean they are cracking down on *dissidents!*"

Braun looked to either side and motioned to Karl to keep his voice down. He had no answer, no adequate response to Karl's assertion.

"I understand," Karl said with resignation, but he really didn't want to understand. The very idea of being willing to understand government policy was preposterous.

Karl realized he was quite fortunate to have a family friend for a defense attorney. He knew that even defense attorneys probably had to be cleared by the government in terms of loyalty to the state. Even if Martin Braun was a party member, Karl thought he demonstrated genuine concern for him. Actually, at best, Braun was only a nominal party member. Justice was of greater value to him than party loyalty.

Noticing that Karl was troubled, Braun leaned forward and patted the boy on the hand. "Karl, I'll do my very best for you. I can certainly speak of your fine family background, your excellent academic pursuits, and your good character."

"I'm grateful, Mr. Braun, I really am."

"I need to ask—would you give any second thoughts to remaining in this country?"

"No! Regardless of what happens at trial, I don't want to stay."

"I see. There is a girl?"

"Yes."

"An American?"

"Yes."

"Your parents seem to think you are very much in love, that you plan to marry."

"Yes."

"You see no future for her here?"

"That's right."

Glancing in the direction of the secret police continuing their stealthy surveillance, Braun lowered his voice. "Karl, if that's the way you really feel, there may be a chance for you through an East Berlin lawyer. He may be able to make arrangements to deliver you to the West."

Karl's countenance began to light up. For the first time in months, he got in touch with a feeling called *hope*.

"True?"

"This is a real possibility. It will take time. You must be patient. That's all I can say right now. Please keep this to yourself. Do not talk about it. Do not write anything about this to anyone, even your family, especially not to your lady friend in the United States. The arrangement is a delicate matter. It must appear as if neither you nor I are initiating the request. I must make a certain contact who, in turn, will make a necessary contact. Understand?"

"Oh yes. Of course. May I ask a question about that?"

"Please."

"When will you know something about it?"

"That's the hardest part of this entire procedure. I don't know how long it will take or when I can give you definite word. Patience, my boy, patience."

"And hope."

Martin Braun gave Karl an assuring smile.

"Now, at your trial, you can help your situation a great deal by not making any political speeches or getting into any arguments if I put you on the stand to testify. And I think I'll need to have you testify. During cross-examination, if the prosecutor or the judge asks you why you want to leave the GDR, simply say you are engaged to be married to someone in the West. Do not mention any other reason. Just don't get political. Understand?"

"Yes."

"I'll see you in court the day after tomorrow. Good-bye, Karl."

"Good-bye and thank you, thank you for everything."

Karl returned to his cell with new material about which to fantasize. He rehearsed his trial over and over. He played out different tactics the prosecutor and Braun might take. The kind of speech before the courtroom audience he was being restrained from making was given in full measure in front of the toilet bowl in his cell. It felt awfully satisfying to get those things said. He flushed them down the drain with a healthy dose of urine and raucous laughter.

The good news about the possibility of being released to the West had relieved a great deal of despair and frustration. Maybe justice would have its day after all. One thing was certain: the courtroom rehearsal was marvelous therapy. He channeled off those burdensome, repressed emotions.

However, there was no way to channel away thoughts of Marlo, which stirred waves of melancholy. He chose to replace the sadness of separation with a mental picture of the time of reunion. He fancied himself making elaborate plans to surprise her with the news of a clandestine release to freedom. His scenario had Marlo's parents arranging for her to be in a special place under false pretenses. *But where? Ah, irresistible San Francisco, of course! There's Marlo, seated at the foot of quaint Lombard Street. I can see the flowers in bloom. She is on a bench, picking a flower . . .*

CHAPTER 21

It was an unusually balmy November afternoon in Santa Rosa. Marlo was sitting on a park bench not far from the family home, soaking up the sunshine. She picked a chrysanthemum in full bloom and gently plucked each petal, watching them drift to the ground. She thought warmly of that December day when she and Karl sat on the bench by the pond at Pillnitz. She pictured in her mind the grand old city of Dresden and the sights of Meissen. And she thought of her introduction to Kurt, Eva, and, Albert. That was nearly a year ago!

Two months earlier, her father had made contact with the executive director of Amnesty International, providing information about Karl Mann. To date, nothing more was known. *The wheels of justice move terribly slow*, she thought.

"Why haven't we heard from Amnesty International?" Marlo had asked her father.

"I'm not sure, but perhaps they prefer to work quietly behind the scenes without tipping their hand. Let's just sit tight and wait to see what happens."

Esther Farrell was busy with plans for Thanksgiving. The Farrells enjoyed hosting family and relatives for the annual observance. Even a few of the aging aunts and uncles graced the gatherings. For the first time in a decade, one particular "uncle" was planning to venture to Santa Rosa from his home in Salinas. Retired Air Force colonel John Stover, whom the family called Jackie, was coming with his new wife, Claudia. Others in the family were eager to see Jackie again and meet Claudia. Stover's first wife, Margaret, had died of cancer soon after he returned from active duty in World War II. They had no children. Soon after they consummated their marriage and he went on active duty, Margaret had a miscarriage. He had remained single for many years thereafter, battling depression caused by the loss of his wife, exacerbated by what years later would have been diagnosed as posttraumatic stress disorder. A military psychiatrist at Fort Ord, not far from Salinas, helped him overcome the dread that plagued his life for years. Claudia, whose husband had been killed by friendly fire in an infantry training exercise, was the psychiatrist's secretary. John and Claudia found the joy of companionship again. Marlo was excited about the upcoming Thanksgiving celebration and to see Uncle Jackie, whom she had not seen since she was ten years of age. She remembered how her older sisters called him their pretend uncle because he was not actually a blood relative. Wesley and Esther had met John as an enlistee at a community soldiers' canteen while delivering homemade cookies. He seemed very lonely. They invited John Stover to their home a number of times before he left for flight training and treated him like a brother. So the Farrell daughters started calling him uncle. But Wesley insisted that they *not* refer to him as their *pretend uncle*. He became affectionately known as their Uncle Jackie.

Even more, Marlo ached to know how Karl was. She lived from one letter to the next sent by Eva Mann. Though never a day passed without thinking lovingly of Karl, she was surprised by the intensity of her thoughts about him just now. As the last chrysanthemum petal fell, Marlo looked at her watch and calculated that Karl was probably going to bed for the night in a Dresden prison.

CHAPTER 22

Marlo, in Karl's continuing fantasy, smells the fragrance of the flower. The sun is warm. She glances up the avenue. Strolling down the winding thoroughfare in her direction is a young man. He looks familiar—the tall, husky blond with a round face. Marlo jumps up with a stunned look on her face. She squeals with joy, runs to Karl, and they embrace and hop around in a circle. For one enormously ecstatic moment, the whole world stops; time itself is suspended. They are together again, never to be drawn apart. Karl gently strokes Marlo's soft, warm cheeks, flicking away her tears of happiness.

There is no way hard, cold, pocked cell walls can feel anything like Marlo's beautiful skin—a rude return to the present moment. Karl held on to the expectation that their reunion would take place soon. The tears to be wiped away had formed rivulets down his cheeks. The cell-block lights turned dim. Karl went to bed. He lay awake, tossing and turning, thinking about his upcoming trial.

There had been little time for Braun and Karl to script the testimony and consider who the prosecution might bring forward to testify against Karl. It left the door open for a good deal of speculation. Karl tried to work out in his mind a number of scenarios. It was unnerving. He fought off the thoughts that streamed into his conscious mind in order to lapse into sleep.

An alarm sounded that alerted inmates that the dimmed lights were about to go out. Pitch-black darkness enveloped Karl. He took several deep breaths and mercifully went to sleep.

CHAPTER 23

The trial date came to pass. The halls of the court building were buzzing with people. Karl was tense, not accustomed to walking in the midst of such a crowd and so much activity. Many months had passed during which Karl had been in isolation behind bars. While one might think he would be elated with this brief respite from the dreary cloister, it was actually a rather traumatic experience.

Shackled to two guards, Karl turned a corner and took a final length of a corridor leading to the courtroom. Footsteps and voices were amplified by the slick marble floor. At the doorway to the courtroom, three figures stood out in the crowd. Karl's visual senses were so bombarded by a plethora of stimuli that the three figures that should have been familiar to him did not register for a moment. Then he suddenly stopped, the spent slack in the chains jerking his uniformed companions by surprise.

"Father! Mother! Albert!" Tears welled up in Karl's eyes.

The three ran up to Karl, embracing wildly and kissing.

The guards realized the futility of trying to break up this family reunion, so they tolerated the interruption and feigned being distracted by others standing nearby.

"We have waited so long to see you, son," exclaimed Kurt.

"Have they taken good care of you?" his mother asked.

"Yes, yes, Mother, I'm fine. It's good to see all of you!"

"Martin Braun was good enough to phone us about your trial date so we could manage to be here," said Kurt.

"He told us what to expect," Eva explained, "and it doesn't look too good." She fought to hold back her tears.

Kurt and Albert comforted her.

"When we received your letter, I just knew it would come to this!" Eva wept.

"Mother, whatever they do to me, it can't be that bad. So they put me in prison for a year or so. Then I'll be free again. They may have my body, but not my mind! Not my heart! Not my soul! I am a free spirit. Please don't worry about me. I'll be all right, I'll be all right."

Kurt was struggling to find a way to change the subject.

"Karl, do you know what happened to our cousin Peter?" asked Albert, who was excited about sharing some news.

Karl shook his head.

"Well, you know how sympathetic he was about people wanting to leave the country. A woman went to his house, asking him to help her leave. I believe he knew her in dental school. I don't know how he did it, but he got her out. About a week later, Peter came home from classes and turned on the television. On the evening news, that *same woman* was being interviewed by a government agent. She was telling about the 'depressing conditions in *West* Germany.' She was a spy, a *spy*, Karl! She trapped Peter."

Karl shook his head slowly in disgust.

"About the same time, he was watching the news story. There was a knock at the door . . ."

"The police came and took Peter away," inserted Kurt. "He's serving a two-and-a-half-year sentence at the Leipzig Zuchthaus [House of Corrections]."

"He won't be permitted to complete dental school," Eva added. "And I worry that they may not let you finish medical school." Eva began to sob again.

Karl cast a forlorn glance at the floor. *Such extreme measures.* "What about Marlo?"

"As soon as we heard about your capture and detention in Berlin, your mother wrote to Marlo," his father replied.

"Soon after, we received a letter from her," Eva said. "I have it here in my purse." She reached for it.

One of the guards immediately stepped forward, thrusting his arm out to halt her. "You are not permitted to give the accused anything!"

Eva flinched.

"What does the letter say, Mother?"

The guard intruded. "There is no more time to talk here! We must go into court."

"Can you just tell me quick what she said?" Karl pleaded.

"She was very upset . . . and . . . concerned about you. She thinks her only recourse now is to come here to live. She wonders if you have been mistreated . . ."

The guards started to pull Karl away and into the courtroom. Kurt, Eva, and Albert followed close behind.

"Mother, please, write to Marlo and tell her"—Karl had to raise his voice to be heard, straining to turn his head—"**not to do anything right now, to just wait. Tell her I am all right. I have not been mistreated. Will you be sure to tell her that, Mother?**"

"**Karl,**" shouted his father, "**we have already written to her and told her to wait. She knows you are now in Dresden awaiting trial.**"

"**Good! Good! Thank you, Father.**"

"**Don't worry, son. We'll keep her informed . . .**" His voice faded in the din of the crowd.

Karl could only manage a smile and a nod as he was briskly taken to his place where Mr. Braun was seated, making some hurried notations on a legal pad. Braun glanced up and greeted his client with a smile and handshake.

The courtroom was filled with government personnel. Also present were concerned friends and relatives of Karl who had had no opportunity to greet him personally. The press and the curious filed in as well. Trials for so-called prisoners of conscience were rather numerous in the 1960s, drawing considerable public attention. Courtroom drama had become a pastime for many citizens.

The judge entered and took his lofty place on the bench. Three jury members filed in to their chairs in a small jury box. Karl began to sense the seriousness of the moment. This was not the drama acted out in his cell for his own amusement or catharsis.

The proceedings soon appeared to be cut and dried. The prosecution had no eyewitnesses to the alleged illegal departure from the GDR but presented into evidence some sworn depositions from his Czech captors.

How ironic, in light of the current international situation, that the court should receive as credible statements the testimonies of Czech authorities, thought Karl.

Surely they are antagonistic toward East German interference. My conviction hangs in **that** *balance?*

The prosecution did present a woman student from Humboldt University who took the witness stand. Inge Vogel was only a casual acquaintance.

"I was shocked to learn that Karl would want to leave our country," Inge asserted indignantly, giving the impression of having been a close friend and confidante of the defendant. "He was always a nice fellow, but I heard him say he wanted to leave."

The prosecutor, also a woman, intimated disgust that Karl, with such a good education and promising career in the socialist system, would attempt to leave.

"And what of Karl Mann's political affinities, Ms. Vogel?" queried the prosecutor.

"Well, I do know he was not enthusiastic about party membership. He kept putting off joining the party. I remember one day in our political science class, Karl was dismissed by the professor for making loud, inappropriate comments."

"Objection, Your Honor!" Braun, interjected, rising to his feet.

"What is your point, Counselor?" snapped the judge.

"The witness has drawn a conclusion about party affiliation not based on fact presented in evidence."

"Objection sustained."

"Your Honor, I will rephrase the question," said the prosecutor.

"Very well. Proceed."

"Ms. Vogel, were you active in any way in student-party affairs?"

"Yes."

"Would you please explain."

"I was the secretary."

"Was a part of your responsibility that of enlisting fellow students to join the party?"

"Yes."

"Had you or any other officer approached the defendant to join the party?"

"I don't know about other officers, but I had approached Karl at the beginning of each term when we held our membership drive."

"And how did he respond?"

"He said something like he was too busy with his studies to get involved in politics."

Braun rose again. "Objection!"

"Yes?" responded the judge.

"This testimony is irrelevant. Student-party membership has no bearing on this case, Your Honor."

"Objection overruled." Turning to the prosecutor, the judged asked, "Do you have any further questions of this witness?"

"Yes, one more, Your Honor."

The judge gestured for her to continue.

"Ms. Vogel, is it not true that your father is Dr. Heinrich Vogel, the distinguished attorney of Berlin who has received a number of rewards by our state?"

"Yes."

"Thank you. I have no other questions of this witness."

The judge peered at Braun over his clutched handful of documents. Martin moved slowly toward the witness.

"Ms. Vogel, I remind you that you're still under oath. We all admire the achievements of your father. Let me assure you of my own esteem for him as a colleague. But of course, your father is not involved in this case. Is it fair to say that you are your own person and not merely your father's daughter?"

"Well . . . yes . . . I suppose so."

"Good, good! Now, you testified that you believed the defendant to be a good person. Is that correct?"

"Well . . . yes."

"Your only concern about Mr. Mann is that he failed to join the party?"

"I guess you can say it was a concern."

"Did you ever hear him make a statement in public that he was critical of our government?"

"Well, if he was not critical, surely he could have joined—"

"Ms. Vogel, please, just a yes or no to my question."

"No."

"Did you ever hear him advocate the overthrow of our government?"

"No."

"Ms. Vogel, did you ever hear Karl Mann intentionally plan to leave this country illegally and show you a *written* plan?"

There was silence.

"Ms. Vogel, do you want me to repeat the question?"

"Oh! No, you do not need to repeat it. The answer is no."

"Well, then, Ms. Vogel, you really cannot find any reason on which to base the defendant's guilt—"

"I object, Your Honor!" cried out the prosecutor. "Counsel is leading the witness."

"Objection sustained," ordered the judge.

Martin Braun strolled back to the defense table to review his pad of notes. "Your Honor, I have no further questions of this witness."

Inge Vogel was dismissed and quickly exited the courtroom.

When Braun's turn came, he brought to the witness stand Kurt Mann, followed by an uncle of Karl and a fellow medical school student, all of whom vouched for Karl's integrity and excellent scholarship. Braun had tried to get one or two sympathetic professors to testify on Karl's behalf, but they declined for obvious reasons of possible governmental retaliation.

Finally, Martin Braun called his star witness, Karl.

"Karl, as you know, you are under oath. This court expects truthful answers from you. Perjury exacts severe punishment."

"Yes, I understand that."

"Karl, have you ever advocated the overthrow of our government to anyone?"

"No, sir."

"In your own words, please tell the court why you did not join the Communist Party at the university."

"I have always been a serious student. I have always felt my studies come first. Anyway, I am not a joiner of organizations of any kind. I just want to become the best possible physician."

"Do you believe that you have received any benefits by living in the German Democratic Republic?"

"Yes, I have received benefits." Karl was glad Braun had phrased the question in that way so he could answer honestly.

"Now, Karl, tell us why you left the country."

"I met an American student who was in West Berlin. She and some other students were visiting in East Berlin. We met in a restaurant. I showed her some of the wonderful sights of our part of the city. We fell in love and became engaged to be married. We believed it would be difficult or impossible for her to become a resident in the GDR. So I decided I would be the one to leave. Then we could have our life together."

"Thank you, Karl. I have no further questions, Your Honor."

The prosecuting attorney stood erect at her table. "Mr. Mann, you admit to leaving this country."

"Of course."

"Did you apply for a visa?"

"No."

"Were you aware that you were planning to leave the country illegally?"

"Objection!" exclaimed Braun.

"Overruled," bellowed the judge. "Answer the question, Mr. Mann."

"I guess I knew that, but I acted on impulse."

"Isn't it true that you do not like our country's politics and you wanted to leave for—"

"Your Honor," Braun protested, "Counsel is harassing the witness. Mr. Mann already explained why he wished to leave and why he did so."

"Madam Prosecutor, rephrase your question."

"I withdraw the question, Your Honor. I am through with *this* witness!"

"You may step down," instructed the judge.

Karl had studied the three jurors throughout the trial. They did not always appear to be paying attention to the proceedings. They seemed preoccupied with their own thoughts when they were not chatting among themselves.

The judge routinely dismissed the jury. Within twenty minutes, the three men returned to the courtroom with a verdict. *Guilty.*

Standing mute before the judge, Karl thought sardonically, *What took them so long to deliberate on my fate?*

"Young man," the judge began dryly, "you foolishly acted on impulse and have brought discredit on yourself. You have violated Article 213 of the penal code: illegal crossing of the frontier. That carries a maximum penalty of five years in the correctional facility. You need time to reflect upon your misconduct and reconsider your allegiance to the laws of the state. This court sentences you to twenty-one months, granting you credit for the three months you have already been detained. Because your intent to take flight as a dissenter has not been proven in these proceedings and because this is your first offense, Mr. Mann, the court is not sentencing you to the fullest extent of the law. This case is closed, the jurors are dismissed, and the court is now adjourned."

Martin Braun extended to Karl his sympathy and gestured the same to his family.

"Karl, remember our conversation two days ago."

Karl nodded.

"I will pursue that matter. One way or another, you will learn the results of my efforts. Good-bye and good luck."

They shook hands, and Braun walked away in conversation with Karl's family.

"A mockery of justice!" Karl whispered. "Ha! Our constitution *guarantees* freedom of conscience, of opinion, the press, the media, religion, assembly, association . . . and . . . let's see . . . oh yes, freedom of movement *within* the country . . . ah, Articles 20, 27, 28, 29, 30, and 32!" Karl had assimilated his reading in the political science class in such a way that his professor would be proud.

But he had also learned about all the snares in which certain freedoms got entangled. Dissenters from the official position were not tolerated. Karl had heard that the law provided for punishment of those who even made or simply talked about making plans to leave the country. Even attempts to emigrate legally by proper application by tens of thousands of citizens had been denied by the government. Individuals who persisted in applying for official permission to emigrate could be charged with defamation of the state or incitement hostile to the state. There were other provisions as well. It gave Karl a headache just thinking about all that.

Karl resigned himself to his sentence, having expected that outcome anyway. While the law provided for an appeal, he knew from his prior consultation with Martin Braun that the court had latitude to set a motion for an appeal aside as being unfounded. They had agreed not to press for an appeal. Their grounds for such a motion were not strong enough in Braun's opinion. And of course, Braun had another strategy to pursue. Anyway, twenty-one months sounded much better than sixty!

Eva and Kurt embraced their son. "Look, don't worry," assured Kurt. "There may be a way to get your sentence reduced by as much as a half by the council of state. Your mother and I will ask Mr. Braun about it. Keep your hopes alive, son!"

"We will write and visit as often as we can," Eva promised. She seemed more composed now.

Albert, misty-eyed, gave his brother a hug. Wiping away a tear, he found it difficult to say anything.

Karl, once again shackled to two guards, walked out of the courthouse, down the steps, and into an automobile waiting at curbside. *Luxury of luxuries!* he thought. His two escorts joined him.

He was surprised to notice that the vehicle was not heading in the direction of the prison on the hill. He asked the officer in the front seat, sitting next to the driver, what was going on.

"You are going to the city jail. You will be there for a few days until you are transferred to the prison at Cottbus."

The car began to slow down as it passed the bombed ruins of the old Dresden palace and the rubble of what was once a Lutheran cathedral. This grand old city still showed scars of the war. These ruins remained as a monument to the ravages of war—a dramatic statement to younger generations of Dresdeners about the folly of waging war.

The vehicle made a sharp left turn and passed through the walled gate of the old city jail. Frequent trips from Meissen to Dresden in his boyhood sometimes took the family by this place. It never occurred to him then that one day he would be looking at passersby from the inside. Karl climbed out of the car and stood in an open quadrangle enclosed on four sides by the tall gray stone building. He went through the usual check-in procedures and found himself sharing a cell with a young-looking boy.

Karl was beginning to like the novelty of intermittent relationships. It was like an oasis in the middle of a very dry wasteland of loneliness. The boy in the cell appeared nervous. He shuffled his feet from side to side and bit his fingernails. Occasionally he glanced up at the hefty figure of Karl.

"Hello! Have you been here long?"

The boy shook his head. "Just got here this morning."

"My name is Karl Mann. What is your name?"

"Richard Schneider."

"How old are you, Richard?"

"Sixteen."

"*Sixteen!* Really?"

"Uh-huh."

"What did you do to wind up in this place?"

"I painted a sign . . . about the government . . . invading Czechoslovakia. I mean, a lot of us students at the school were angry about this."

"Did many of your school friends get caught?"

"I don't know. Not many . . . I think maybe some did. I haven't seen any of them here. The police came to my house early this morning and brought me here."

"Well, Richard, it looks like we are what you call prisoners of conscience—what the authorities call criminals. So they put us in jail with every kind of common criminal you can think of."

"You painted a sign too?"

"No," Karl laughed. "But if I had been with you, I would have borrowed your paintbrush and added a word or two to your sign! No, I did something else just as bad according to the law. I tried to leave the country without permission. I got caught. So here we are."

"Ohhh."

"Where is your home?"

"Here in Dresden."

"And you have a family living here?"

"Just my mother."

"Any brothers or sisters?"

"No."

"I'm sure your mother will come to visit you."

"Maybe. She works in a flower shop."

"Do you know yet when you will go to trial?"

"No."

Karl felt sorry for the boy. He walked over to the bed where Richard was sitting and gave him a hearty pat on the back. "Look, Richard, I know things look bad right now. There is a possibility that you will not be convicted. But if they do, you will not serve a full term. After all, you're only a youth, and this is your first offense, right?"

"I've never been in trouble before. I'm scared."

"Yes, well, the end of all this will be here before you realize it. You'll be all right, believe me."

"I've never been away from home before. I've heard bad things about being in jail . . . I mean, I've heard what older ones in here do to kids."

"Look, if anyone gives you problems, you just ask to talk to the boss around here. And you tell me. I'll help you."

"Okay." Richard appeared much more relaxed. "I wish I could have a Bible to read."

"Ah, you could read worse in this place!"

"I've never been religious or gone to church much."

"Maybe religion is the only thing you can trust anymore. God can't be happy about this!"

"I wish God would come here and help."

"Well, maybe God has. We are here together to help each other."

Karl's encouragement seemed to give Richard a lift. His posture shifted upright. The muscles of his face loosened. Karl spent the remainder of the day coaching Richard on the mental ritual he had been using to help him keep his sanity though he was careful not to use the word *sanity* with the boy.

Several days later, Richard had his appointment with the court. Late that afternoon, he returned to the cell bawling. He collapsed on his bed and buried his head in his arms. He was embarrassed to be seen crying but couldn't hold it back. Karl stood in the corner and silently looked on for a few minutes. Then he went over to Richard's bed and sat down. He slowly reached out and gently rubbed the boy's back and shoulders. After a while, Richard's weeping subsided.

"Do you want to tell me that happened?"

Richard sat erect and wiped his blotchy red eyes. "I got convicted."

"And?"

"Three . . . and . . . a . . . half . . . years!"

Karl cast about in vain for some wise word, something of comfort to say. He concluded that silence was the better choice. He just put his arm around Richard and continued to massage his shoulders and neck. *Three and a half years for simply painting a pro-Dubček slogan on a sign! God, he's just a boy! The government just wanted to make Richard an example to other youngsters.*

In spite of the fact that Richard's mother lived locally, two days later, Richard was taken to a prison some distance from Dresden. Karl would not see or hear of Richard again.

A little later that morning, Karl was ushered out of his cell and taken to the jail barbershop. The barber gestured for Karl to get into the chair. "How would you like it styled?" the barber taunted as he proceeded to give Karl a complete buzz cut. Karl felt humiliated. If that were not enough, the introduction to his first shower was traumatic. Several inmates were made to stand in a single file outside the gang shower on the tier. In turn, each prisoner undressed in front of a guard who was seated on a stool. There was a pause before each one moved from the front of the line and into the shower room. Karl was puzzled by the delay with each inmate before him. Then his turn came.

After Karl removed his clothing, the guard's eyes narrowed as he looked up at Karl and ordered, "Move closer." With a perverted smirk, the guard began fondling his genitals. Karl was mortified. His cheeks flushed angrily as he jumped back.

"Stand still!" demanded the imperious guard. "I'm looking for bugs."

Karl felt degraded by the egregious act. Defiant, he stomped forward.

With nostrils flared, the guard said with disdain, "I thought you had VD. *Your kind* usually do." He squeezed Karl's scrotum then slapped it against Karl's leg. A smile of delight crept across the guard's face as he witnessed his subject grimace. "Now you can go to the showers."

Karl's few days in the city jail lengthened into weeks. The experience of lining up for a shower was repeated once each week. Steeling himself from total humiliation and brutal threats was a whole new world of experience and adjusted behavioral reactions that sapped his emotional energy. Yet he remained intrepid as he kept focused on his goal to achieve freedom, if not simply survival.

That objective was pursued just one day at a time. Karl felt he could manage a twenty-four-hour block of time.

He was relieved that he now had his cell to himself as he adjusted to his new reality. It was the world beyond the walls and bars that was illusory now. It took some wild mental gymnastics to produce this kind of perception, this armored shield to protect an otherwise vulnerable psyche. The exhaustion that hit him at the end of each day mercifully induced long hours of sleep.

At times Karl waxed philosophical. *This prison world is a good training laboratory for becoming a physician. I will become sensitized to all manner of human travail that will limp into my medical clinic. Perhaps I could specialize in psychiatry.*

Shortly before Christmas, Karl was to be visited by his parents. Conflicted feelings welled up within him. On the one hand, seeing his parents again and getting the latest news of the outside world, which included news of Marlo, would be wonderful. But on the other hand, his parents would intrude upon his new real world he had made such an effort to construct. The holiday season brought a relaxation of the rules so he could visit with *both* his father and mother at the same time for thirty minutes.

In a glass visiting cubicle, under the watchful eye of a guard, Karl sat across an empty table from Kurt and Eva. He sat in a fog of detachment.

Eva's voice sounded distant. "Marlo wrote that she will wait for you as long as it takes. She has a part-time teaching position. Would you believe, she teaches German." Eva laughed.

"Son," reported Kurt, "Martin Braun tells us some encouraging news about a covert effort to get you released! Albert has a job driving a taxi in Dresden."

They asked about his life in jail. Karl spoke in wooden tones. When the visit ended, he remembered little of the conversation. Gift exchanges were not permitted. They were allowed to say farewell with an embrace.

Later, Karl had a faint memory of something having been said about plans to obtain his early release. However, those thoughts went through a diabolical metamorphosis, a sinister taunting. He was happy to hear all was well with Marlo. However, living only one day at a time provided no space for some future hope.

When Christmas Day came to that illusory world on the outside, it was just another day in Karl's real world. Yet the fact of Christmas could not be kept from breaking in upon his consciousness. Entertaining the memory of Christmases past and of family in this present world of captivity became depressing. Though he did not allow himself to think it, deep in his heart of hearts, he knew his family's home was only a few kilometers way. And he also knew the struggles through which he had passed that made it possible to excel in medical school. Now the Communist government of East Germany might take that away from him.

CHAPTER 24

Karl, half asleep in his cell, continued to think about his challenging medical school experiences. His dormitory on Borsigstrasse was a dark—gray stone building with blotches and streaks of white as if someone had indiscriminately splashed whitewash to brighten an otherwise dreary facade. Though tall and muscular, he labored to carry his luggage up three flights of stairs to his room. The cubicle was small, containing a bed, an armoire with one leg shorter than the others, a secondhand easy chair with foam stuffing bulging out of splitting seams, a reading lamp, a desk that had a missing drawer, a desk stool, a few bookcases over the desk, a wash basin, and a toilet. The showers were down the hall. Actually, he was being housed in the Evangelisches Konvikt, living quarters for theology students.

He found the demand for excellence was persistent in medical school. Courses were not unlike those in other European and American medical colleges. Except for the cost of textbooks and supplies, medical education was free. The government supported universities through taxes. In Karl's mind, however, there was a price to be paid—*giving up the freedom of voicing one's opinion, traveling wherever you wish, contributing a pound of flesh to the political system. I'm not sure that's a good trade.*

Pressure from faculty and upperclassmen was constant in terms of overtures to join the Communist Party. Students had to concoct incredibly outlandish excuses not to sign up.

One student demurred, "Oh, I'm not well enough educated in the virtues of the party and program to be a leader in the party that has a historical responsibility to chart the course for the German nation."

Karl compressed his lips into a thin line and suppressed his laughter. *I wonder how much time he took to think that one up and rehearse it!*

"You must know," came the predictable rejoinder, "that as a physician, you will not be eligible for such a position as chief of medical services in a hospital or professor of medicine in a university. Only those committed to Marxism can truly lead our country, and they are the ones who deserve positions of leadership. That includes medicine. You say you want to be a Christian? All right, we will tolerate your opinion, but we won't support you for advances in your profession."

Though feeling very much like second-class citizens, the students who resisted official party affiliation seemed to number in the majority. Dissenters learned to keep quiet.

Karl understood why Marxist-Leninist Communism was presented so thoroughly in elementary and high school and now in college. The government's strategy was to ensure that all people were properly indoctrinated as to why they lived in political circumstances that necessitated austerity in order to motivate acceptance, and to explain that the benefits of Marxist socialism are only possible by repudiating the evils of Western capitalism cloaked in democracy.

Students like Karl had few opportunities to openly discuss or debate political notions of those who touted Marxist socialism as *the* hope of the future. He discovered the need to be extremely careful with whom he spoke regarding politics. There were some individuals on campus appearing to be students who were actually members of the East German secret police. However, the Christian Student Youth Movement on campus was an arena that invited a free flow of ideological conversation. Usually students who opposed the government or socialism and appreciated the advantages of dialogue congregated in this organization. Over time, Karl could single out those who shared his aspirations for individual liberty.

Karl's reminiscence took him further back in time to an incident that occurred in high school. His classmate Walter had been officially barred from enrolling in any expanded secondary schools of the republic because of his obstinacy about a sensitive patriotic issue. Soon after the Berlin Wall went up, government authorities went into the schools to talk with the children in their classrooms about the reason for the wall. Its construction had been a major political event for East Germans, even for high school students. Following a presentation by government workers, pupils in Karl and Walter's class were invited to respond with what they thought about the wall. The question-and-answer period was designed to discover what kinds of things were being said in the pupil's homes. Not a word was spoken. They had learned not to be critical or even raise innocuous questions. *Besides*, as Karl recalled, *the future of our education depended on our behavior, our attitude.*

When the government people left, the teacher said, "You must say something the next time they come!"

"They're coming back?" asked Walter.

"Of course! They have more information for you. Next time, don't appear so stupid, so disinterested."

The following week on the day of the officials' return, early in the morning before class, one student had sneaked into the building and taken down all the pictures of Stalin. They were thrown into a heap in the school yard. Walter got into his classroom early and wrote on the chalkboard, "We don't like the wall. We don't like Russian rule."

The school principal was irate. The culprit who dismantled the pictures could not be identified. But someone saw Walter nervously leaving the classroom and reported him. Walter became the scapegoat for the whole affair, which embarrassed the principal in the presence of the government representatives.

At a meeting of all the students in the school auditorium the following day, Walter was made an object lesson. He was publicly ridiculed and humiliated in the presence of his peers.

"You have brought disgrace upon your fatherland. You have brought disgrace upon your whole family. You have brought dishonor upon this fine school. You have brought discredit upon your fellow pupils. Your childish, unpatriotic behavior will cost you dearly. You are hereby expelled from the school." The principal was most severe in his manner and speech. *I never saw Walter again. I wonder what happened to him . . .*

His next mental picture was of an occasion at the medical school refectory at noon. Karl remembered joining some friends around a table in the corner of the hall.

"What's the matter, Rainer, no appetite?" Karl had quizzed sardonically. He noticed how his friend had reacted to the class's first exposure to a cadaver *before lunch.*

Rainer had given an inaudible grunt, staring down at his coffee cup, stirring it nervously.

Karl remembered that others at the table muffled their laughter.

Karl was not repulsed by the appearance or feel of the dead body. In fact, he felt a close kinship to it; they were like partners in learning medical science. He could enter the pathologist's laboratory and watch an autopsy without flinching.

Rainer took their taunts in stride. "It's just that . . . well . . . *that body* . . . it reminded me of someone I knew."

"Great Aunt Marie maybe?" Joachim offered whimsically.

Rainer shook his head thoughtfully. "But it's a strange feeling when you're working on a corpse you think you once knew as a living person."

There had been an uncomfortable silence around the table.

"Are you going to political science class today, Karl" Joachim had asked.

"I think I'd better. I've missed a few sessions lately. I'm behind copying class notes."

"Two hours a day, each day. That kills a lot of time." complained Joachim.

"I agree," replied Karl. "I could use that time in the library or catching up on my lab experiments."

Karl figured that about one-third of his medical school education was devoted to studies of history, politics, and economics of Marx and Lenin. One hour each day was spent in tutorial—about one hundred students in an auditorium listening to a lecture by the instructor. That was followed by seminars in which the larger class was divided into smaller units of about twenty students. Knowing the instructor frequently gave surprise exams based on lecture notes put pressure on everyone to be in class. They knew if they ever needed to apply for a scholarship to pursue advanced studies in an area of specialization, their grades in political science would have to be high even if their grades in medically related subjects were passable.

Karl did not appreciate sitting through a lecture on politics without being able to raise questions. Those for clarification were allowed. After all, the objective of government-paid education was that the students were to learn something important about their national life and not to confuse one another by questioning the merits of the system.

That afternoon following the conversation over lunch with Joachim and Rainer, Karl walked into the political tutorial to face one of those surprise exams.

"Dr. Pfeiffer," Karl had protested, "I do not think we should have to take *this kind* of an examination."

The professor looked at Karl sternly. A hush quickly came over the auditorium. The outburst was startling.

Karl continued, "I think college students should be trusted to attend class on the merits of the interest and challenge what the instructor offers the students in presenting the subject matter—"

"I did not give you permission to speak!" Pfeiffer interrupted angrily.

"I will *not* take this examination!" replied Karl. By this time, his hostility was unmasked.

"What is your name?" demanded the professor.

"Karl Mann." The words rolled off his lips adroitly.

"Well, Karl Mann, you must leave the room. I will talk with you later in my office."

Every eye in the auditorium was trained on Karl as he marched out.

There were students in that auditorium who silently praised Karl for his guts to say what many of them felt. Joachim winked at Karl as he passed by.

Later that afternoon, Karl stopped by Pfeiffer's office.

Peering over his thick-rimmed glasses, Pfeiffer said, "Ah, yes, Mr. Mann, I believe."

"Yes, sir."

"Well, come in and sit down."

"Yes, sir."

"The issue you raised in class today is something I cannot discuss in class. We are not there to challenge policies, procedures, or subject matter. We are there to learn . . . in the best Germanic tradition."

"I understand. I'm sorry, it won't happen again." Karl was more fearful of expulsion than being contrite.

"I'm pleased to hear you say that, young man. Your—shall we say—uncontrollable outburst will be written up in your file, noting that disciplinary action has been taken. That will be that. Any further incidence like this may lead to your dismissal from medical school. That would be a pity, Mr. Mann, for I see that you are one of our best students. You may go."

As Karl left the faculty building for supper at the refectory, he thought about the dossiers kept on the students. Their attitudes toward party membership, participation and grades in political science, and their activity related to elections were charted about as closely as an attending physician charts the pulse, blood pressure, food and fluid intake, and waste discharge of a patient!

Each summer, the university students were required to participate in a military program. To refuse meant automatic expulsion. Karl and others reluctantly went off to summer military camp. Issued old worn-out uniforms and equipment, the students spent much of their time playing war games and being motivated to possess patriotic zeal.

"Enough! Enough!" Karl called out from his cot. *Too many memories come flooding back. My brain is ready to explode.* Finally, he sought escape through sleep with chimes from a nearby church pealing a soothing lullaby.

The only thing *new* about New Year's Eve, he learned from a guard, was the promise of new quarters. Karl was about to be dispatched across the countryside to Cottbus on a special train.

January 1, 1969, found Karl and numerous other inmates herded onto a train and shackled to their seats. God help them if the train were to derail with no chance of being released from bondage to flee from such wreckage! With only one car for guards and two cars for prisoners attached to a diesel engine, the train moved swiftly across the landscape north a hundred kilometers to the intended destination.

Chapter 25

In one respect, the Cottbus prison was like most others. A high wall surrounded the complex of buildings, with guard towers perched on top at intervals around the perimeter. But there were differences at this facility that Karl had not expected to encounter. Once inside the main building, it was apparent to him that this prison was a walled work camp. Without windows, corridors were kept almost totally dark except for an occasional subdued blue light. A single white line painted on the concrete floor was the only hint of a direction in which to walk from one location to another. The hallways were arranged in a zigzag pattern throughout the building to thwart any inmate's attempt to move quickly in the maze. Interior guards monitored corridor zones from fixed camera feeds.

Prison officers processed Karl in an intake room beyond the first sally port. His photo was taken. He was fingerprinted and then stripped naked and fumigated as a precautionary measure. Since his hair had grown out during his Dresden incarceration, Karl was given another buzz cut.

Karl's clothing and personal belongings were placed in a locker, and he signed the inventory slip to be placed in his file. He was subjected to another indignity as he was ushered into the adjoining infirmary for a cursory physical examination that concluded with a body search for contraband.

"All right, spread eagle and bend over," snapped the medical assistant. Karl swallowed hard and grimaced as the examiner stuck what felt like his entire hand up Karl's rectum. He was placed in a holding cell and given a white jumpsuit to climb into. *Two insufferable years in this place! And for what! For simply wanting to cross the border and start a new life elsewhere.* Karl realized that to have legally petitioned for expatriation, he would have had to stage a melodramatic episode with signs of being on the verge of an emotional breakdown if he could not identify a close relative with whom he would live in the country of destination. He had heard of such antics. But to whine and whimper before condescending authorities with their puffed-up hubris did not appeal to him. The whole thing seemed so ludicrous, though not amusing. He was haunted by the thought that, once released from prison, he may not be able to finish medical school and become a physician in East Germany. There were no guarantees. It felt like a lose-lose situation.

"You'll have to remain in this holding cell for a day or so until you are classified for a job," explained an officer. "Then you will be assigned to your own cell."

With my background in medicine and having been an orderly, surely they will assign me to that kind of work. Karl sat on a bed in the corner of the cell, sorting out his thoughts about this new set of circumstances. To survive for two years, he knew he would have to adapt.

Karl was shaken out of his thoughts by the slamming of the cell door. A guard released a young man, very slender in form, from the manacle and pushed him into the cell. Obviously despondent, this new arrival shuffled to a chair and dropped himself into it. He appeared unaware that Karl was there. The stranger sat rubbing his face slowly with his hands. Karl sat quietly observing him. Then he looked up to see Karl. He decided not to speak. He wondered if the other occupant might be a spy planted by government officials intent upon coaxing valuable information out of him. Anyway, he didn't feel in the mood to talk with anyone. He glanced at Karl again. Karl nodded with a smile.

"Hello! My name is Karl Mann," he spoke softly.

The fellow simply sat there with a flat affect and said nothing. He sensed a welcoming gentleness in Karl.

"What brings you to *this* resort hotel?" quipped Karl.

Finally, Karl's new cell mate broke the awkward silence. "I tried to cross the border from Koper to Trieste and got caught. You know, from Yugoslavia to Italy."

"Yes, of course. You are East German?"

"Yes."

"Well, I also got caught trying to leave the GDR. That's why I'm here."

"My name is Hans Heinrich."

"Where is your home?"

"A farm near Görlitz, on the Polish border."

"Ah yes, that's a wonderful ancient walled city."

Hans nodded.

"I'm from Meissen. What is your line of work?"

"I recently graduated from engineering school in Dresden and was working at a manufacturing plant in Zittau." Hans began to speak with more animation. "What about you?"

"I have been a medical student at Humboldt University."

"I've spent the last several months in a Dresden jail."

"So have I! In the secret-police prison?"

"Yes. And also in the city jail."

"Interesting!" exclaimed Karl. "We must have been up on the hill at the same time."

"I suppose we were."

There followed a period of silence. Hans studied the cell and its accoutrements. He spotted a chessboard on a little wooden table. "Do you play chess?"

"Yes. And you?"

"It's been a long time."

"Want to give it a try? It's one way to keep our minds off our troubles, eh?"

"A chess game is like trying to escape to the West . . ."

Karl cocked his head to one side, trying to comprehend the statement. "Do you want the white chess tokens?"

"That's fine."

"Good! I like playing defense."

"What I mean is," Hans went on to finish his point, "you never know the way to victory in advance."

"I see your point."

"You think you've eliminated your obstacles, only to be backed into a corner and—"

"Checkmate!" Karl nodded.

As they began their series of strategic moves across the board, they felt a rapport developing between them. Hans disclosed his elaborate escape route from East Germany to Bulgaria and scaling a mountain into Yugoslavia. "And I was so close to freedom, maybe a hundred meters from Italian soil."

"What happened?"

"A hound on a leash linked to a long wire was sprung from a cage. He caught up with me and clenched his teeth into the cuff of my trousers. I couldn't move. I was put in a Yugoslav jail and eventually extradited to the GDR. I almost escaped from the Yugoslav jail."

"How did you manage that?"

"No bars on the windows. Using a thin coin, I unscrewed the latticed metal interior window covering. But when I jarred open the glass window, sunlight glanced off the glass and awakened the sleeping guard outside my cell. That shaft of light hit him directly in the face!"

"What made you want to leave the country?"

"The Vietnam War. I was a student protester against our involvement with the Viet Cong. And the Warsaw Pact troops rolling into Czechoslovakia. I am *opposed* to militarism and Marxist Socialism and what all of that is doing to our country! My family's farm has suffered terrible consequences of government farm policies. The farm co-ops are a disaster."

Hans paused to consider his next move. *A knight or a bishop or castle my king?* He captured one of Karl's pawns with his knight. "Did you protest the GDR's military interventions too?"

"Not really, though I don't like war either." Karl went on to tell his story.

"I had a girlfriend too, Marie. I tried to talk her into leaving the country with me, but her parents exerted a lot of pressure on her to stay. She was too attached to her family. We ended our relationship."

The chess match brought to a close a long afternoon. Karl was the victor. After a meager supper of soup, bread, and coffee, they retired for the night.

CHAPTER 26

A steel-gray dawn over the city of Cottbus unimpressively broke through the window of the prison's holding cell. Hans was already awake. As if orchestrated, lights flashed on everywhere in the building, and the noise of prison employees simultaneously brought a six o'clock overture to another day. Karl began to stir, frowning to forbid the bright lights from penetrating his closed eyelids.

"Hey, Karl!" Hans gargled, clearing his throat.

"Yah," Karl grunted as if still half-asleep.

"Maybe today we move out of this cell, huh?"

"Don't know."

"Does Marlo know you're here?"

"My parents wrote to her about what happened since my capture. I think she knows by now."

"I wonder if Marie knows . . . or even cares to know."

"Hans, don't think about her. Just think about getting out of here."

"Ha! This place has tight security."

"That's not what I mean. I mean getting out *legally.*"

"That's so far-off, I don't think I *want* to think about it."

"Well, I have a feeling something's going on. I mean, our release may come sooner than the length of our sentence."

"*Really!* For you, maybe, but not for me."

Karl chose not to push the subject any further. He simply took comfort in knowing, from what his father had briefly related to him, that their attorney-friend, Braun, had a colleague in East Berlin, a certain Gustav Arndt, who in turn had a contact with a West Berlin lawyer. Between the West Berlin contact, Amnesty International, and the Bonn government, some set of complicated procedures were to be put in motion that could lead to the early release and probable expatriation to the West. Karl thought the chances were good for Hans or any other prisoner of conscience to pursue the same objective. He made a mental note to explore the possibility on Hans's behalf the next time he had a visit with his father or Attorney Braun.

Breakfast was brought to the holding cell. A hard-boiled egg, a roll, coffee, and tomato juice was the bill of fare. The guard entered, looking very solemn. "Karl Mann and Hans Heinrich, after you eat, you will be taken to your permanent cells and work assignment." The guard turned and walked out. The cell door clanked shut and locked.

As promised, the two were ushered out of the holding cell. Guards took them through the dark corridor and system of sally ports to an adjoining cell house. They were happily surprised to find themselves to be in cells next to each other. Because an armed guard patrolled their tier, passing by at frequent but irregular intervals, it was difficult for them to converse. Visiting between cells was discouraged. A whisper could not be heard between them. Karl and Hans did not want to jeopardize their being housed so close together, so they concocted a scheme of communication by tapping an alphabetical code on their connecting toilet plumbing. A very light tap could easily be heard through their toilet bowls. The pool of water in each bowl was an excellent conductor of sound. The clink of the tapping did not seem to carry down the tier. When they heard the footsteps of a guard, they had time to stop tapping.

Testing their communication system helped to make the day pass. They were never approached about their work assignment. Karl kept hoping it would be something to do with health care. Hans wondered if the prison authorities would acknowledge his specialty of agricultural engineering and assign him to food production if they had an area in the yard to raise fresh produce. So—*tap tap tap tap tap*—they shared with each other their imagined work scenarios.

The following morning a guard stood at Karl's cell to march him and other inmates on his tier to the dining hall for breakfast. "Come!" he said sternly. "You must eat your breakfast and report for your work assignment."

Karl stepped into the single file. Hands of inmates were to be clasped behind their backs until they reached their assigned tables for meals. Hans was in line behind Karl. The morning meal had to be consumed within a fifteen-to-twenty-minute time span before going to their respective jobs.

The food was nothing to write home about—rather bland and starchy. But mealtime really became a social event, a time for conversation with other inmates. Karl and Hans, assigned to the same table, cherished these opportunities.

Two of their tier guards came to Karl and Hans. One accompanied Karl to a work assignment director. Hans disappeared in the company of the other guard, presumably to meet with his job counselor. Karl entered the assignment director's office. The guard motioned for Karl to sit.

"Karl Mann?" the director intoned laconically without looking up from his paperwork.

"Yes, sir."

"You're assigned to the machine shop."

"Machine shop!"

"Exactly."

"Are you aware I have medi—"

"Report now!" he sneered with an air of self-importance, thrusting a pointing finger toward the hallway outside his office.

"But—"

"That's all, Mr. Mann," he said, his eyes riveted on the prisoner for the first time.

The guard lifted Karl up out of the chair and guided him to the shop. The shop supervisor met him at the door.

"I am Max Busch, the supervisor of this shop," the beefy figure in the doorway said with an air of insolence. "Be on time and do your job right, and you'll get no trouble from me. Have you ever worked a metal press?"

Karl, frozen in startled dismay, shook his head.

"Well, you'll learn fast enough. Here's the instruction manual. Read it tonight. Be ready to operate the machine in the morning. For now, tour the shop and become familiar with what's here. Talk to no one." Busch pivoted on his heels and swaggered away. With speechless astonishment, Karl stood at the doorway.

"Go on! Do what he said," ordered the guard. "I'll wait here. When you're finished, report back here to me. I'll escort you to your cell."

Karl walked through the shop, observing inmates operating various contraptions he had never seen before. He was curious about what they were making but remembered he was not to speak to anyone. Later he was taken to his cell, where he looked through the metal-press operations manual.

Ha! Karl thought to himself, *change the design of these machine parts and it might work wonders for brain surgery . . . or maybe adjusting the attitude of Max Busch!*

For thirty minutes in the late afternoon, Karl, Hans, and others had access to the open-air exercise yard for basketball, handball, or jogging around the fence line. Then to the showers.

At dinner that evening, while spooning a bowl of potato soup, Karl talked about his experience at the machine shop and asked Hans about his work assignment.

"Nothing in food production. I'm assembling parts of photographic equipment."

After dinner, they filed back to their cells with nothing to do for entertainment.

"Say, can you get me a chess set?" Karl asked a guard.

"I'll see what I can do about that tomorrow."

Ten o'clock. Lights out. No talking. "Morning comes early," reminded a guard on the tier.

Each successive day began at six o'clock. The daily routine tolerated no variations. Inmates spent nine hours at their jobs. There were weekly "educational" meetings with his counselor, Wilhelm Kafitz. Eventually Karl got his chessboard—without chess pieces, however. He molded the different shapes of the pieces out of bread he took from the dining hall. He stained the opposing pieces with grape juice in a cup he also confiscated. He enjoyed playing both sides of the board. Of course, he never lost a game!

Chapter 27

Another day, another week, another passage of lost time. Another breakfast not unlike the very first and those that followed.

"Hey, Karl!" Hans was animated with obvious excitement. "Do you realize that tomorrow we will have been in this place a month? *Thirty days?* Do you know what that means?"

Karl sipped his coffee. "I'm sure you'll tell me."

"We're eligible for a visit!"

"Ha! Whether it's the first or the tenth, you get to talk with *one* visitor for an entire *fifteen minutes*," scowled an inmate seated across Karl and Hans. "*Fifteen minutes a month*! Isn't that generous! They know where they can stick their high and mighty visiting regulations!"

Hans and Karl had made up their minds long before this day not to engage in negativity. There was an abundant supply of cantankerous yelping. It was tempting. It was contagious. But it was not healthy. They gave a polite ear to the inmate's sarcasm without encouraging him further, then continued their conversation.

"Are you expecting your father or one of your brothers, Hans?"

"My counselor brought me a letter Friedrich wrote last week—"

"Oh yes, *big brother* lets us send one letter out and receive one letter a month," interrupted the other inmate bitterly. "That is, after it's read and approved by the secret police."

Karl nodded to Hans. "Go on."

"Friedrich said he would drive my father here for a visit. Maybe tomorrow or the next day. What about you? Any word from home?"

"I got a letter from my parents. I think they'll be here around the first of next month."

"I suppose we can live for our visits one month to the next," Hans said wistfully, trying to convince himself more than anyone else.

They were dismissed from the dining room for their shift on the job. As Karl approached his mechanical companion in the shop, he reached into his pocket for the homemade earplugs fashioned out of cotton and paraffin. His task was to push a button on a metal-press machine, and the air-pressured mechanism would slam down on its metal base with a loud metallic thud. It was a boring job. *Well, at least it's better than sitting in my cell all day. I can only play so many games of chess!*

Max Busch was making his usual inspection of the machinery before the daytime shift began. "Passable," he said condescendingly, "passable. Mann, remember, you are responsible for this machine. Otto [Karl's counterpart on the night shift] did not do the best job cleaning up the mess here." Max pointed to metal scraps on the floor. "It had better look clean when you are finished!"

If any good came out of Max's bellicose nature, it was that Karl was learning restraint. The assertive medical student, capable of challenging a university professor on political science issues, would not fare well in this environment.

As Max Busch strode away, Karl, his cheeks flushed with anger, silently watched and climbed onto the seat attached to his machine. He reached down and placed his hand on the clutch, squeezing the V-shaped handle in order to shift the clutch into the operative position. Karl slowly drew in a breath and exhaled. He experienced a sudden flashback—lying on the ground by a fence and squeezing wire-cutters. It seemed so long ago. He shook off the intrusive memory and focused on the task at hand.

CHAPTER 28

On the doorpost of a fashionable office building on Lenin Allee in East Berlin was a shiny brass nameplate on which was etched "Rechtsanwalt G. Arndt" (G. Arndt, Attorney-at-Law). Gustav Arndt had practiced law for thirty years, growing professionally with the new republic. He was a staunch defender of Communist principles. Like Dr. Heinrich Vogel, Arndt had won the admiration and acclaim of the heads of state in the GDR. With numerous awards came a posh lifestyle, which Arndt willingly flaunted with expensive clothes and a handsomely polished Mercedes—one of a very few owned and driven in East Germany.

As an official member of the East German diplomatic corps, Arndt played a key role as a broker for expatriating prisoners of conscience. He and his counterpart, Erik Holschuh of West Germany, worked out exchange agreements between the two governments sub rosa. Both governments were always prepared to deny the unwritten but official policy designed to benefit both countries. Gustav Arndt found himself in a rather powerful position of aiding his republic in the pursuit of greater economic strength through bargaining.

Gustav sat at his desk, impatiently waiting for Erik's arrival, puffing and chewing on his cigar. He poured himself another cup of coffee, looking at the massive early-eighteenth-century antique floor clock that graced his lavish suite. It was ten twenty-five. He brushed the dandruff from his dark-blue pinstriped silk suit. Masterful in the art of political survival, of raw survival as a matter of fact, he was a man to be reckoned with. This was particularly true if one was not prompt for an appointment. He interpreted lateness as an exercise of control, of power—something Gustav felt privileged to use as his own device but did not tolerate coming from somebody else.

A buzz drew Arndt to the office intercom. "Your ten o'clock appointment is here, Mr. Arndt," his secretary informed him.

"Please show Mr. Holschuh into my office." Arndt pulled his portly frame out of the chair, drowned his cigar butt in the remaining pool of coffee, and lumbered toward the door. The secretary opened the door, and Erik Holschuh entered.

The West German attorney flinched as he strode into Arndt's office. His nostrils had been invaded by the stench of stale cigar mixed with strong coffee. The foul odor pervaded the room, making the air seem heavy.

"Ah, Erik, come in, come in! I was wondering what was keeping you."

"Good morning, Gustav. Forgive my delay. You have new guards on duty at the subway station who are not accustomed to my weekly visits. They detained me with their meticulous investigation."

"Ah, so!" Arndt chuckled for a moment. "Well, let me grab my file, and we shall take our usual walk, eh?"

The two lawyers began their stroll down Lenin Allee to a quaint little café on Schillingstrasse.

Holschuh was a middle-aged barrister who earned his doctorate degree in England. He was a quiet reformer by temperament, with his own unique capacity for political survival and diplomacy.

He was well liked and trusted by the Bonn administration and was a Western European contact person for Amnesty International—an organization that won his respect when it had disclosed the whereabouts of an incarcerated relative held incommunicado behind the Iron Curtain some years earlier. Erik's credentials made him a heavyweight for dealing with someone as imposing as Gustav Arndt over such sensitive matters as liberating political prisoners. These days, it was a full-time chore.

Over coffee and cheese strudel, the two men reviewed dossiers of twelve persons imprisoned in East Germany—nine men and three women, eight of whom were students. All of them, according to the court records, unequivocally wanted to leave the German Democratic Republic.

"What, only twelve this week?"

"Yes, our government is reducing its quota for the moment," Gustav replied with a faint smile.

"You disappoint me. I thought perhaps your government had closed hunting season on dissidents!" There was a twinkle in Erik's eyes.

"Erik, you won't complain when you see what I've brought you. There are three prize catches in today's collection," said Arndt as he pushed the files from the stack and brought them to rest in front of Holschuh.

"Well, my friend, you know very well they must pass my government's criteria. Will they be productive workers, and do we have assurance that they are not—"

"Future spies planted by our government?" interrupted Gustav with an irascible demeanor.

"Your words, Mr. Arndt, your words." Erik reached out and patted Gustav's arm.

"I believe their dossiers speak for themselves." Gustav lighted up a cigar. "Go on, take a good look." He sucked on the cigar until he achieved a sustained red glow that emitted thick smoke around the table. He knew his cigar smoking was an annoyance to Erik. It was a part of Arndt's "diplomatic" game plan—a tacit assertion of leverage.

Erik never complained about the stinking odor of the cigars. He was not hesitant, however, to signal his displeasure by taking his napkin and waving it about to disperse the white-gray fog elsewhere.

Erik studied the materials on the three. One prisoner's name caught his immediate attention—Karl Mann, an honor student in medicine. *Amnesty International had posted that name on a Teletype*, he remembered. There was another medical student, Fritz Schimmel, with excellent academic marks. "Hmm, this one looks good as well—Hans Heinrich, the graduate in engineering near the top of his class. All of them . . . attempted escape . . . none of them sympathetic with government reforms . . . no prior criminal record . . . hmm." Holschuh looked quite satisfied with what he saw on paper.

"I thought you'd be pleased with what you saw in those files. Their price is thirty thousand Deutsch marks."

"Thirty thousand for the three—"

"*Each*, Erik! Thirty thousand *each*," he said, tapping his forefinger assertively on the table. Gustav flicked cigar ashes into a tray and gave Erik a nod. "Of course. Just think of it as an investment. A good risk, I should say." Gustav rolled the cigar back and forth in his finger and thumb, staring coyly at Erik.

Holschuh looked through the remaining dossiers. "And these?"

"The usual."

"Antibiotics? What your government can't obtain from the USSR?"

"That's what I mean."

"The foreign ministry has the final word, of course. After they have reviewed these and rendered a decision, I will let you know."

"Spare me the formalities, my friend. I know all that."

"Just for the record, Gustav. God knows I get tired of making the same speech over and over again." Erik knew as well as Gustav that either or both of them could be bugged at any of their clandestine rendezvous.

"Erik, I know your foreign ministry relies heavily on your recommendations just as my superiors rely on mine. Just don't be too particular. After all, our people's economy will get a real boost from your currency. And you get some of our fine products of East German education!"

"You don't have to remind me about the value of our marks in your GDR banks! We know your prison releases are not exactly prompted by altruism. And you're getting a hefty supply of scarce medicines."

Arndt grinned broadly, straightening the fresh boutonniere in his lapel. "Erik, you and I always get something of value. Sometimes you have East German prisoners to release into our custody—"

"But not this time. Marks and medicines trump prisoner releases."

"Well, we practice a good balance of trade, eh?" Gustav Arndt slapped his hand down on the table, causing dishes to jiggle. He guffawed, shaking his rotund body.

"I suppose that's one way to put it." Erik smiled politely.

"It appears that both of our countries have their hands full of young radicals defiant about Vietnam. They learn well from the imperialists!"

"Yes, Vietnam . . . *and Czechoslovakia!*" Erik fixed his eyes on Gustav's countenance.

Arndt hastily pulled out his gold pocket watch and read its face ceremoniously. "Eh . . . I haven't time to talk politics now . . . must get back to the office for another appointment."

Holschuh let the issue rest there, content that the opinion score was even. Gustav's body language indicated that Erik had him almost cornered with his rejoinder.

Having finished their coffee, pastry, and verbal sparring, they walked back to Arndt's office. Their conversation transitioned to small talk about the weather and inner-city development projects. They bade each other farewell until the next week.

Both men secretly enjoyed the company and banter that the weekly conferences provided. These occasions added a bit of delightful surcease to an otherwise intense fare of Machiavellian jurisprudence. Ulterior-motivated compromise, in which principles could get mangled, was no respecter of political philosophy, be it democracy, socialism, capitalism, or communism. Ethics and a moral compass are just as easily hung on the coatrack with hats and coats outside the door to the smoke-filled rooms where foreign-policy decisions are crafted.

Holschuh was warmed by the feeling that if their respective governments could speak to one another even indirectly in this enterprise of human commerce, albeit in surreptitious fashion, there might be a happy future for the German peoples now divided by a sharp political divide, a massive wall, and high fences near buried land mines.

After all, Erik mused, *over the centuries of Germanic history, how many times has political geographic boundaries shifted? Given time, patience, and the strong will of all Germans to preserve a common heritage, Germany might one day be reunited.*

Erik felt great satisfaction in his mission. In spite of Gustav's rather impersonal, mechanistic approach to their task, Erik thought that there *was* indeed altruism at work here, a humanitarian concern. This effort just might be a link—however small—in a long chain of events and relationships that would one day bring about a united Germany. This thought gave Erik a sustained purpose for his life and work.

The svelte attorney emerged from the U-Bahn station on the west side of Berlin's wall and walked with a quickened step toward his office near a government building.

"*Principle, principle, principle!*" Gustav Arndt reiterated with emphasis as he sat alone in his office. "Erik is always bringing up some idealistic principle. He sneaks it in so as to disarm you."

Gustav gestured a salute to an imaginary companion across the room. "I have to hand it to you, Erik. You are a clever fellow! You see how you leave me with these thoughts?"

Perhaps there is more charity here than I'm willing to admit, Gustav said more privately within himself. *Yes, there was a dreadful viral epidemic two years ago . . . and a shortage of antibiotics. I would have surely lost my sister if it had not been for a shipment of drugs from Bonn. That supply saved many of our people. I'm grateful for that! Bonn could have refused us medical assistance, but it didn't. We could have traded with the Soviets at a much higher cost and more strings attached, but we didn't. Germans looked to Germans for help. Germans responded to Germans in need.*

It was rare that Gustav permitted himself to reflect on such ideas. A strange and wonderful warmth came over him—a feeling he did not experience a great deal, one that he had perhaps denied for much of his life. He basked in it for a time, fondling his gold pocket watch while it remained harnessed in his vest pocket. He became mesmerized by its muffled rhythmic tick.

Chapter 29

The time had come for Karl's February visit, his second opportunity since entering the Cottbus prison. After his working hours, he was led to a visitor's room. Karl's father was waiting there. As usual, Karl's assigned prison counselor was present to monitor the quarter-hour visit. Father and son embraced affectionately while the counselor tried to appear disinterested.

Kurt held his son at arms' length for a moment. "Son, how have you been?"

"I'm well. The work is long and hard, but it keeps me well occupied. At least I know I'm not cut out to be a camera manufacturer." They laughed.

"Your mother and Albert are well. You should be receiving a letter from your mother soon."

"And what do you hear from Marlo?"

"She is fine, son. We correspond regularly. Her family has taken quite an interest in your situation. How is Hans?"

"He's doing very well, in fact, much better than when he first arrived."

Kurt noticed the counselor's momentary distraction by something taking place outside the visiting room and seized the opportunity to share something in a subdued voice.

"Karl, your mother and I have worked out a way for you to receive direct correspondence from Marlo." He stopped for a minute and gave a casual glance in the direction of the counselor. It appeared safe to continue. "We have sent Marlo blank pieces of your mother's writing paper. Marlo will write a message to you, and then your mother will complete the remaining space on the sheet of paper with her own message. Your mother will try to make her cursive characters look like Marlo's. So read your letter for this month carefully to detect Marlo's message."

Karl arched his eyebrows in wonder. "But the secret-service officers scrutinize our mail."

"Let's hope they only scan and don't examine the contents and penmanship that closely."

"Does Marlo realize I can only receive one sheet of paper with writing on both sides?"

"Yes. We encouraged her to write small. You know, your mother has small handwriting anyway."

"What a great idea! I hope it works. I want so much to hear from her." Karl tried to conceal his emotions. "Did I tell you that I tried to get Marlo on my approved correspondence list but the authorities denied the request? They said I can only hear from my lawyer and one relative."

"No, we didn't hear about that."

The counselor's attention seemed to shift back into the visiting room. The topic of conversation changed.

"I haven't heard from Mr. Braun since Christmas," Karl said.

"I have some good news for you, son. We heard from him just the other day. He said that the GDR Berlin lawyer had given your records to a lawyer in the Federal Republic of Germany. We should be hearing something about your case soon, maybe before our March visit."

"I hope Hans' case will also be considered."

Kurt shrugged his shoulders. "I'll see what I can find out and will let you know."

"Anything exciting happening these days in Meissen?"

"Oh, not really. Everyone is about the same. Folks ask about you. I bring you greetings from Mr. Lenz, you know, Rudolph Lenz, who has the bakery down the street. He and Annie ought to give up the bakery. They're getting on in years." Kurt chuckled spontaneously. "The other day, Rudolph was telling me about an electrical problem in their apartment upstairs. He told me he had been trying to get an electrician to his home for *two weeks*. The electrician wants assurances that Lenz has the money to pay in advance of the repair. But he said"—Kurt broke into laughter again—"he said, 'The electrician never comes, and the Communists never leave! What kind of world is this anyway!'"

Karl and his father looked at the counselor, wondering if he heard Rudolph's comment. Apparently not.

"What was that you wrote in your last letter about an educational program here in prison?"

"Well, I meet with Mr. Wilhelm Kafitz here, my counselor, once a week for discussions. The meetings are mandatory. He discusses what appears in my correspondence, which he sees, and what he observes in my visits. If I write something improper in a letter, he will suggest how I ought to rewrite it so it will be acceptable for mailing. He asks me to read various *approved* books and articles to reeducate me for a more compatible life in the German Democratic Republic when I'm released. He tries to help me understand that my future happiness and success as a citizen in our country will depend upon a constructive, conciliatory change in my attitude and behavior. And I have a chance to talk about my working conditions." Karl was careful to use a tone of voice that would not betray his disgust with the program.

As he talked about this, Karl recalled an experience Hans had had with his counselor not long ago. That counselor repeatedly questioned Hans about his motive for escaping. He frequently tried to trick Hans into making politically disloyal statements. One day, Hans apparently had stated very candidly, "I do not recognize the GDR but only East Germany and West Germany as *one* Germany!" The counselor went into a rage.

Karl thought too about how some guards were known to smuggle cards and letters out of the prison for a good price. Sometimes Karl wished he had enough money to yield to that temptation in order to communicate, without the censoring, directly to Marlo. But now he rested in the happy prospect of hearing directly from her through the method his parents devised.

"Have you heard or seen anything of Fritz?" Kurt inquired.

"No. I've watched for him in the dining room and in the shop. The last I saw Fritz was in the Dresden prison. I asked Mr. Kafitz if Fritz was here, but he said that information is not given out. I figure that if he isn't here, he must be in the Bautzen prison."

"I understand they move prisoners around from one place to another. So he might have been here at one time and was moved or perhaps be moved here from another place sometime later."

"You have just five more minutes," Kafitz announced.

"Son, your mother and I love you. Albert too. He keeps watching the store for me. We will keep writing and visiting."

They reached out to each other and grasped hands. Their misty eyes met for a moment. A bit embarrassed, they looked away simultaneously.

"I love all of you too. I'll keep writing."

Kurt Mann was shown out of the visiting room and through a sally port. When that door was secure, Kafitz ushered Karl along the corridor to the dining room, where he joined Hans at a table.

"Hans, I just had a visit with my father. Everyone is well, and I should hear from Marlo soon."

"Good! I expect my brother, Friedrich, to come this Saturday. I got my February letter from my father today. All seems well with him. Since there is little activity at the farm these days, he is really in retirement—forced retirement. He and his old friend Otto will have more time to play pinochle."

"My father gave me some hopeful news about the possibility of an early release."

"Good luck! Speaking of release, do you know Max Leinsdorf?"

"Who around here doesn't! He's the one who has been in prison since 1963 for writing 'Soviets, leave the GDR' on the walls of several buildings."

Hans nodded. "Word is, he's going to be released tomorrow!"

"Think of it—six long years. *Six?*"

"He had to serve a full sentence."

"Rumor is that he was quite a radical, and prison only embittered him."

"A law student. Probably no future for him now. Poor fellow," Hans lamented. "Say, Karl, I finally got my clearance to attend chapel service on Sunday. It took *four weeks* to get a reply!"

"I know. At long last, I got mine also. I think the delay is a way of discouraging chapel attendance. After all, the government doesn't value religion."

"I'm looking forward to going. It'll be a welcome diversion from the usual daily routine," asserted Hans.

Karl agreed.

When Sunday afternoon arrived, Karl and Hans were surprised to see how popular the chapel service was. "It looks like there are about two hundred crowding into this confined space," noted Karl. "Look at that! Others with permits are being turned away at the door. Standing room only."

"My guess is that they won't allow anyone to stand. The prison administrators could care less that they've issued more permits than available seating will accommodate. Karl, I think it's a ploy to deliberately discourage anyone from attending."

Inmates were required to take their seats before the arrival of the clergyman, who entered and later exited from another door at the far end of a separated chancel. There were strict rules to obey.

Standing before the assembly, a guard said, "You must not have any physical contact with the minister, and you shall not talk to him. You shall not state any opinion in the service. If you do, you shall be removed immediately, denied future chapel attendance, and lose certain other privileges."

The name of the Lutheran minister was never known. The same cleric conducted the weekly services. There was speculation that he had been incarcerated in a Nazi death camp during World War II, perhaps at Buchenwald, and had been, like martyred colleague Dietrich Bonhoeffer, a dissident having denounced Hitler. It may have escaped the intellect of prison authorities that such a clergyman would be sympathetic to these present-day dissidents. At least the inmates at Cottbus, who filled the chapel room to capacity each week, felt as though he was something of an icon of faith and courage.

Prison rules prohibited singing or music of any kind. The only congregational vocal participation allowed was the reciting of prayers. When the Eucharist was celebrated, the inmates had minimal contact with the minister. A guard stood next to the priest as inmates filed by to take the wafer and dip it into a chalice of wine. Even the cleric was not above suspicion for passing or receiving contraband.

A platoon of guards ringed the perimeter of the room, conspicuous in their uniforms with large name tags that spelled out the guards' identification numbers—no names. Guards addressed each other only by number in the presence of inmates, careful not to disclose their identities.

Prisoners with numbers. Guards with numbers, Karl thought. *In twenty months . . . maybe less . . . I will be out of this place. These guards will remain. Who is the **real** prisoner anyway!* That gave him some consolation.

Karl sat on the hard bench, scanning the chapel. His eyes suddenly fixed on the profile of an inmate seated at some distance from him in the front row. The facial features appeared very familiar. *It is Fritz!* How Karl wanted to call out to Fritz. How he wanted to reunite with his medical school buddy. Karl kept staring at Fritz, hoping that Fritz might pick up on the vibes and glance back.

During the service, Karl's mind was flooded with memories of experiences he and Fritz had shared—preparing each other for college exams, the merriment of Oktoberfests, the rendezvous with American students at the Lindenkorso Cafe, their flight through Hungary and Czechoslovakia, the tall grassy meadow and the fence . . . and yes, the dogs. The thought of the dogs sent a chill through his body. The *dogs!* There had been many nightmares about being chased by dogs, being mauled by ferocious hounds, being devoured by savage beasts. He would never feel comfortable around dogs again.

As his stream of consciousness returned to the room, Karl found himself gripping the sides of the bench until his knuckles were white. Beads of perspiration had broken out across his forehead. Remembering the dogs was too much for him.

Again he focused on Fritz—or at least, the fellow who looked a great deal like Fritz. Karl's body and mind became relaxed. He hoped for a chance to see this man at close range. If indeed it was Fritz, Karl hoped for a chance to speak with him after the service.

That hope proved futile. Inmates were marched out of the chapel, starting with the back row. Karl exited the area before anyone in the front row would start moving out of the room. Karl would wait for another opportunity to make the connection.

CHAPTER 30

Howling winds and torrential rain were nature's introduction to April. Karl approached the metal-press machine on a Monday morning, oblivious to his supervisor's glaring stare.

Grabbing Karl by the shoulder, Max Busch shouted stridently, "Karl Mann, clean up that mess under the machine!"

"I cleaned up after myself Saturday when I left my shift. That's not my mess," Karl retorted, pulling away from Max's grip.

"Look, idiot! Don't argue. Do what I tell you, dog, or I'll knock the—"

"You don't have a right to call me names! You don't have a right to threaten me!"

Max Busch glowered.

"I'll write a complaint to the secret service and my lawyer."

Busch had great difficulty containing his rage. He looked around the shop and noticed others were witnessing the confrontation. Karl turned aside and mounted the seat of the equipment. He inserted his ear plugs and started to work, ignoring the pile of metal shavings on the floor. His supervisor stood by like a trembling volcano ready to explode, his face red with a demonic expression.

Inmates like Karl learned quickly the prison's pecking order—the vulnerability of those at or near the bottom—and how to use the system in order to survive. A bluff or not, the mention of filing a complaint, the use of words like *lawyer* and *secret service* evoked a good measure of angst in lower echelon staff.

Although the long day's work shift had brought the metal-press machine to a temporary cessation, Karl's body typically continued to jolt with a series of aftershocks, and his ears were filled with the usual echoing *bang bang bang*. Predictably, he collapsed on his bed for another night of sound sleep.

The day following the episode with Busch, Karl was summoned to his counselor's office. Kafitz began, "Karl, what is this I hear about an altercation between you and your supervisor yesterday?"

Karl explained what had transpired, insisting he had been unjustly belittled and reprimanded.

"Now, Karl, don't you think you overreacted?"

"No, sir. This isn't the first time he's harassed me."

"Perhaps Max was not himself. After all, everyone is entitled to a bad day."

Karl was mute, looking down at the floor and shaking his head slowly but deliberately.

"Look, Karl, adapt to your situation! Life is not always fair. Be a model prisoner! You're a professional, so be a leader among your fellow inmates."

Karl said nothing.

Kafitz began to pace the floor. "You know the rewards: you may watch television—"

"I don't care to watch television, thank you. I just want to go to my cell."

Kafitz had little tolerance for such obstinacy. Karl was not at all mollified by the counselor's patronizing gesture.

"Before I go to bed," Karl said, "I want to write a letter to my attorney and to the secret-police commander of this prison. I want them to know of this situation. I know I have this right."

Wilhelm Kafitz gave Karl an appraising look. He knew by law he was not permitted to read letters of complaint. He also realized he had to deal carefully with Karl because a memo had come across his desk only a few hours earlier stating that this prisoner was eligible for an early release. He gave Karl pencil and paper to write his grievances while in the counselor's office.

"Your letters will be delivered," Kafitz assured him.

As time passed, Karl never received a formal reply. But he noticed one day that Max Busch had been transferred out of his shop. Karl never saw him again. He took satisfaction in believing that his protest had something to do with the supervisor's absence. Karl felt good that he was not utterly powerless. Maybe there was hidden within the prison system a humanitarian spirit after all. To be sure, it *was* humiliating for a future doctor to press a button on a metal-punching contraption. Nevertheless, his life mattered. A tyrant had been banished. As a captive, Karl was *free*. Quite possibly, he had saved fellow inmates from aggravation at the hands of the abrasive taskmaster. Such thoughts were comforting.

CHAPTER 31

Easter Day, Wilhelm Kafitz called Karl to his office. "I am not sure our education program over these many months has served to direct your thinking toward an improved life in our great republic."

Karl made no response.

"Yes, I've received your records. I know what you said at your trial about eventually leaving our country." Wilhelm paused and looked up at Karl, searching for some reaction. Karl did not oblige.

The counselor resumed. "You really ought to stay in this country of your birth. We will get you back into the university to complete your medical education. We will provide you with a pleasant apartment. Why? Because we recognize you as a brilliant young man. Our society can benefit from your promising medical career. Think of the number of ill and disabled people in the GDR you will be able to help, many being among your relatives and friends."

Karl had heard this speech before. He learned from friends that such promises were often broken by vindictive authorities. A part of him wanted to believe Kafitz and would delight in serving the health needs of people he knew in East Germany. He felt a twinge of guilt about deserting them. And then he quickly thought of Marlo.

"I have already decided to leave, and I have my reasons."

Impatient and angry, Wilhelm slammed Karl's dossier down on the desk and drew himself up briskly from his chair. Turning his back on Karl, folding his arms, and cocking his head erect, Kafitz stared out the window. There were a few minutes of silence.

"If you won't cooperate with us," Wilhelm intoned ominously, "you cannot expect to get any support from our government!" He was bitter about losing this case. That would place his career in jeopardy. His job security and upward mobility was dependent upon the rate of success in rehabilitating prisoners assigned to him. He felt he could not afford to lose this case. It was becoming clear he could not break through Karl's stubbornness. He assumed Karl did not know yet about his pending release should he not accept Wilhelm's offer. Finally, Kafitz waved Karl off without turning around. "Go, get out of my sight!"

Saturday, May 4, Karl was ready to march to the mess hall for breakfast before reporting to work when an officer pulled him out of the ranks as the others marched on.

"Karl Mann?"

"Yes, I am Karl Mann."

"Take all of your things from the cell and come with me."

Karl was puzzled but dared not ask questions. *Is it possible I'm leaving the prison? Did Braun score a victory for me?* He refused to entertain the thought further, not wanting to get his hopes built up only to be dashed down in utter disappointment. He rummaged through his meager possessions in the cell and began to carefully, slowly place his sculpted chessmen and the board into a duffle bag.

"Forget that! We don't have time to stow all of that!" grunted the officer as he knocked the chessmen and board to the floor.

Karl looked on in amazement. As he studied the fallen chessmen, he noticed with interest that the heads of the king and one of the knights broke off and tumbled away. *Maybe that's a good omen,* Karl thought, forming a thin smile. *Maybe that represents the demise of the Ulbricht and Honeker Communist regime that will one day surely come.*

He found himself being taken into a section of Cottbus prison he had never seen before. It was a wing of office suites well secured behind a series of sally ports and armed guards. The soldier escorted him into a spacious, well-appointed suite. Karl breathed in the aroma of freshly brewed coffee. Karl's well-trained analytical mind led him to surmise that he was in the office of a high-ranking secret-service officer. The distinguished-looking gentleman who sat circumspect behind the desk confirmed Karl's hunch.

The man was indeed the top-ranking officer of the elite secret-service corps. Without a word, he gestured for Karl to take a seat positioned directly in front of the desk about six feet away. He waived off the soldier who accompanied Karl. Looking around the room, Karl saw a bank of windows along one wall that looked out into the Cottbus landscape. On the opposite wall was a large window open to the hallway and within view of an armed guard. When the officer rose to his feet behind the desk, Karl felt overwhelmed. It seemed to Karl that the officer was at least seven feet tall!

"Karl Mann, do you know why you are here?"

Of course, Karl's fondest hope was that he would be released soon and expatriated to the West. But he wondered if the complaint he had written might have led to this meeting and some consequential disciplinary action. *Perhaps I'm going to be transferred to another prison. They may see me as a troublemaker and need to get me out of here. I hope not! I'll miss seeing Hans and finding Fritz. How should I answer the question?*

"Ah, I really do not know, sir."

"You are going to be released soon, Mr. Mann. When you are released, what do you want to do?"

Until now, Karl had had no difficulty stating adamantly his desire and intent to leave the GDR and make a new life for himself in Western Europe with Marlo Farrell. This time, Karl found it difficult to get the words out. The officer's announcement was unexpected, leaving Karl in a state of shock.

Nevertheless, Karl said forthrightly, "I want to leave the German Democratic Republic."

"To bring good German stature to one of our allies, of course—Poland, Romania, Bulgaria perhaps?"

"To be very honest with you, no."

"I thought not. It is to the West as I suspected."

Karl couldn't believe what he was hearing. "Ah, excuse me, sir. What did you say?"

"You heard me correctly, Mr. Mann. Arrangements have been made for your release. You are going to the West. I have reviewed your case. What a pity! You have so much to offer your fatherland, which has given you a splendid education made possible, of course, by the generous policies of the Socialist Unity Party. We need men of your outstanding capacities. The GDR deserves a return on its investment in you." But he knew full well by the report folder before him that a certain Gustav Arndt had sealed an investment return in valuable West German marks.

Karl was ready to burst with delight but restrained his emotions for the time being.

"You know, of course," the officer continued, "that when you leave the country, you will not be able to return. You will not see your parents or brother again."

"When will I be leaving?"

"Within a day or so."

"May I phone my parents and tell them what is happening?"

"No, that is against prison policy. Besides, your attorney will probably notify them."

"I would like to have a chance to speak to them . . . to hear their voices when they learn I—"

"I suppose you weighed that possibility against your wish to leave your homeland."

Karl searched for an adequate rejoinder but came up empty.

"Mr. Mann, you will be taken to a holding cell in preparation for your release. Good day." The officer gestured to a guard outside the office to enter and take Karl to the holding cell.

He found himself in the presence of four inmates inhabiting the cell. They too were bound for the West.

When Hans Heinrich returned to his cell block after his work shift, he noticed Karl and his belongings were gone and another inmate was occupying the cell. *Karl is going to be released to the West just as he predicted. On the other hand, he may be transferred to another prison to complete his sentence. I am happy for Karl if he is being released. But I am sad we did not have a chance to share some parting words.*

Speaking aloud as if Karl were present, "Karl, there is so much I want to say to you. I'm grateful that you lifted my spirits when we first met. You became such a trusted friend. I will miss you. Good-bye and good luck."

The following day, Hans appeared at the holding cell. He and Karl could not hold back their shouts of jubilation. As soon as Hans entered the cell, they embraced.

"Karl, did you know?"

"Well, not for certain. But it did occur to me that if I was going to be released to the West, you would be also. I had given your name to my parents and asked them to pass it on to the East German lawyer. I never got confirmation. Apparently, though, that's what happened. How I had wanted to tell you about the plan, Hans, but it would not have been fair if it didn't turn out well for you. I was not even all that certain about myself!"

The dam broke. They wept. The stress of nearly a year of confinement washed away.

Other inmates gradually joined the six. Now, with arms full of personal belongings, there were twelve, huddled tightly in the cell. Seemingly out of character, the guards' demeanor was casual and friendly. Food was remarkably improved—*sausage* for breakfast! The twelve were amused by the abrupt change in the manner by which the authorities were treating them. If there continued to be even a trace of doubt about their imminent freedom, this new gentility would certainly allay it.

The sun had reached its zenith, casting warm rays through the window of the holding cell. Then two secret-service personnel approached the eager dozen.

"Follow us. You are being transferred to another place to be prepared for your eventual destination of the Federal Republic." As they stepped out of the prison building, they nearly choked at the smell of a dense metallic odor that prevailing winds occasionally sent from the coal-mining operation nearby.

The twelve were loaded into a small van—not the caged variety they had experienced before. The comfortable little bus with seats for everyone took them into the countryside, heading south.

After a while, one of the inmates asked, "Do any of you know where they are taking us?"

Everyone looked at the others, shrugging their shoulders. "I have no idea," someone said.

Hans and Karl looked at each other with a look of wonder. "Well, all that I know is that we are being taken to a place to prepare us for a transfer to West Germany," replied Karl.

"Do you think they are duping us?" another asked.

"Who knows? I have been deceived enough times that I don't trust what they say to us," someone else asserted.

Finally, another said, "Karl-Marx-Stadt."

"Oh, Chemnitz!" another exclaimed. "That's close to my home!"

CHAPTER 32

The pungent fragrance of springtime was something of which even a bus could not deprive its passengers. It lifted their spirits with new hope for their future.

"Karl-Marx-Stadt!" a soldier announced to the inmates as the bus came to a halt.

Ha! The city of Karl Marx! What an insult to old Chemnitz! thought Hans.

The compound at Chemnitz, a former World War II military camp, was nothing like a typical prison. Yes, there were armed guards patrolling the grounds enclosed by a high fence. But there was a distinct difference. The atmosphere was relaxed and hospitable. There was a small inmate population. Karl and Hans were able to share a room, which was locked at night.

When they gathered in the dining room for a meal on the evening of their arrival, they found a bill of fare unlike what they had known for a year or more—a good variety of meats, vegetables, and fresh fruits. The inmates were told they could come to the dining room whenever they wanted for snacks—coffee, tea, cakes, fruits.

There were no assigned jobs for any of the arrivals. A game room was at their disposal for cards, checkers or chess, or just lounging to read East German newspapers and periodicals or watch television. The guards who circulated were quite friendly. It was like being in a whole new world. *This is like going to youth summer camp,* Karl thought.

They could spend the day in their rooms and sleep if they chose. That was a real luxury, especially with *soft pillows*—something unknown in prison. They could even shower at will *without* being watched. Nothing seemed to be regimented.

The subtle strategy of the East German government became clear to Karl. The inmates' last impression of the GDR's hospitality was intended to be pleasant. Their pallor betrayed a year of poor nutrition and restricted time in fresh air and sunlight. Ample food and unlimited time on the grounds were designed to change all that. If it were not for the great temptation to indulge in that which had been denied them for so long, Heinrich, Mann, and several others commented that they would have remained pallid for the free world to see. But that idea faded in the presence of a need to be fulfilled. They were like a herd of cattle being fattened before slaughter. No, it was more like being fattened for a propaganda display to the West. The ghost of their former selves, aided and abetted by prison austerity, was indeed slaughtered with all evidence of that murder eliminated.

The inmates got dangerously reconciled to this new life of leisure. Two weeks had transpired, and neither Karl nor Hans were restless. Their psychological defense was in peril. If the government had one final shot at wooing the prisoners or trying to dissuade them from leaving the country, this was it. The authorities were masters at playing on submerged guilt and fear. Occasionally it worked. And when it did, the East German government headlined it in its propaganda.

Certainly there were attractive incentives to cool the passion of would-be defectors. "Look, you just join the party by signing here, showing your patriotism," they would say, "and we will make an investment in your future. Because of your decision, your act of loyalty after you have gone through so much, you will be rewarded, and we will help you begin a new life. We will provide you with housing and find you suitable employment. There will be a note of indebtedness against your name, which you can pay off over a period of time to fit your budget at low interest rates. For each child you bring into the world, we shall grant you a bonus that will reduce the principal of your debt substantially. It is quite possible for you to have enough children to completely cancel your debt!" Such was the casual comment of a mild-mannered high-ranking officer whenever he had an audience of inmates around him in the popular game room. The spiel was not unlike what party promoters told students from high school through college. This government policy was general public knowledge.

Karl reflected at length upon this incredible about-face treatment by prison authorities. He had experienced severe treatment in Berlin, Dresden, and Cottbus. It was degrading and dehumanizing. And now those in charge of the Karl-Marx-Stadt facility were congenial and generous almost to a fault. Karl was reminded of some things he learned as an orderly in the Dresden mental hospital. A therapist had been lecturing workers on the ward one day about personality disorders, a more neurotic but less severe type of mental disability. He had said that throughout life, one will encounter people whose behavior is a definite pain in the ass but about which little can be done to change from destructive to healthier ways of interpersonal relations. He pointed out that people with personality disorders are not motivated to change through therapy. Some exhibited compulsive behavior. Others were what you call passive-aggressive, and so on. But Karl was beginning to think that perhaps these theories that pertained to individuals could be applied to human organizations, systems, corporate personalities. This flip-flop behavior of prison and government officials seemed to be something like a personality disorder, bordering on total derangement. *How can those holding positions of authority possibly live healthy lives, performing in such an equivocal way day in and day out?* he wondered. It was a real challenge to Karl's analytical mind to bring some kind of rational, reasonable interpretation to what he had been experiencing. *Does social, systemic dysfunctional behavior lead to individual personality disorders, or does the latter compound to cause organizational disorders? Or is it some of both?* Karl wrapped his mind around those ideas.

The following day, Karl was summoned to meet with a secret-service agent. He received the final pitch each and every inmate got, including Hans the day before.

"And keep in mind, Mr. Mann," the agent concluded, "you don't know what the future holds for you in Western Europe. That's a whole different world. It holds many uncertainties and risks. You may not be trusted, and so doors of career opportunity may close in your face. Competition in the medical field will be intense. Not so in our country. We offer guarantees. Your opportunities here are almost unlimited. You know your way around. You will be close to your family."

"No, I know what I want. What I really want is not here."

"We will discharge you tomorrow, and I am happy about that. You must sign these release forms declaring no legal claims on property, inheritances, or possessions of any kind except what you have with you."

Karl signed the document. It was immediately notarized. "I will not be happy if you release me to the GDR."

"What would you do if you were?"

"I would apply for a visa."

"That is not possible, not with a prison record."

"Then I would try another way."

"Escape?"

"If I must. Until I am successful."

"Mr. Mann, it is obvious to me that there is no useful place for you in our society. You *will* go to the West. You are making a foolish mistake."

Karl, thinking of Marlo, could only grin. But he quickly realized it was a bittersweet decision he had made. The sweetness was an exhilarating feeling of victory in achieving his goal at last. It had been a long, hard road to freedom. The sweetness was the prospect of seeing Marlo again in the very near future.

The bitterness? A sense of finality about relationships that had been a part of his life from earliest childhood memories—family, relatives, friends, familiar haunts around Meissen, picnics along the Elbe, the cultural stimulation of grand Dresden. What was so ironic was that the government left him no choice, yet it was his signature on a piece of paper that brought closure to much of what had given meaning and character to his young life. There was irony too in the finality coming in the brief stroke of a pen after an attempt to depart by way of an arduous, gallant, time-consuming journey.

Some grief clutched his heart. This final break with relationships was more difficult than he had expected. It reminded him of friends whose marriages had ended in divorce. Was his grief something like that? he wondered. This hard-won victory was taking place without any fanfare. There were no assemblages of family, friends, and dignitaries. There were no flags waving or bands playing. It was a sobering kind of leave-taking.

Nagging self-doubt found its place on the stage of drama. What if the officer was right about the competition in medicine being tough? Supposing Marlo has lost interest in him by the time they get together again? What if they get married and the marriage does not work? He'd be cut off from the emotional support of his family and friends. Karl had to shake himself. It wasn't like him to have his self-confidence eroded. He got things back in perspective.

Karl was clear about his priorities. He was willing to accept the consequences that accompanied his choices. He sensed he was learning some valuable lessons about real life that perhaps he could not learn in any other way. His love for Marlo was compelling. His hunger for freedom was enormous. These greater values propelled him into an open future and the unknown.

Saturday morning, the last day of May 1969, burst forth with dazzling sunlight. Excitement filled the air. The cheery songs of a variety of birds—this was nature's way of providing for bands playing and flags waving to set the stage for a triumphal exit from the GDR. A dozen political prisoners were about to be expatriated, among them Hans and Karl. They all were busy browsing through the stacks of discarded clothing in the supply shop.

"Get what you need quickly! The bus is ready to leave," shouted a guard from the doorway.

There was little time remaining to try on anything to see if it fit. Karl clad himself with trousers and a sweater that was rather stretched out of shape and gathered a few items into his duffel bag. In payment, he parted company with the last of his currency, leaving him with no cash when he got to West Germany. Hans found himself draped in a baggy suit. He relinquished his remaining five hundred East German marks. He found a few other things, including a new pair of shoes, to stuff into his hand-me-down suitcase.

The twelve climbed aboard a worn-out vintage world-war bus for a free ride to the border. Hans fixed his eyes on the city-limit sign the bus was approaching after leaving the prison grounds. "Karl-Marx-Stadt . . . Karl Marx . . . Is that a touch of irony, Karl, or what? I mean, here we are, leaving a prison as political prisoners in an East German town renamed after that Russian rascal. And his birthplace is in Trier, the Federal Republic of Germany! Any loyal GDR Socialist would have grave difficulty trying to make a pilgrimage there. Here we are, getting a free ride to the Federal Republic! He and Karl giggled over that.

On the edge of Eisenach, only twenty-eight kilometers from the border, the bus pulled over into another roadside rest area. The passengers were allowed to get out, stretch their legs, and use the toilet. Hans thought it providential that they should stop for a rest at that particular location. Off in the distance, standing above the town of Eisenach, was the Wortburg Castle. The late afternoon sun, now behind the castle and trees, cast the historic citadel in sharp silhouette. The three, along with the others, clustered together at the roadside, looking in silent vigil at Wortburg, which was a symbol of freedom to many religiously oriented individuals in Germany. They remembered how Martin Luther, a Protestant Reformer, had gone into hiding at the Wortburg in the sixteenth century in order to escape the excesses of the Vatican. It was there, under the assumed name of Knight George, that Luther surreptitiously translated the Bible into the German language. A courageous act in those days!

The dozen reflected on this legacy of freedom of which they were now grateful recipients. They thought prayerfully about many prisoners of conscience they were leaving behind. It was a heady moment, a moving experience.

Soon they were on the road again. When they came to the last East German town of Herleshausen, within a few kilometers of the border, the bus came to another stop along the side of the road.

"We will wait here until the exchange bus from the Federal Republic arrives," said the driver.

It was almost dark when a bus coming from the West swung into the large parking area and stopped alongside the waiting passengers. Several plainclothesmen on the other coach received their new charges. The plainclothesman who had been riding with them from Karl-Marx-Stadt also joined the twelve on the Federal Republic coach. He seemed to be giving some sort of signal to his peers that this was a bona fide payload and all were present. The West German bus driver lost no time revving up the motor, peeling a hasty U-turn out of the parking area, and moving toward the border.

Hans turned to Karl and quietly confessed, "You know, Karl, I was never really sure if this trip was taking us to freedom. It is only now, *right now*, that I can accept the fact that it is true. It is not a dream or my imagination or my suspicion that it was a cruel hoax of the GDR."

Karl stared at Hans intently, silently. An imperceptible nod with closed eyes registered Karl's acknowledgment of similar feelings.

CHAPTER 33

Karl and Hans were so overwhelmed by their transfer into what one other student dubbed the Freedom Bus and wheeling ever closer to the border that they scarcely realized they were riding in a new luxury motor coach that they had never set eyes on before. It was a Mercedes with a toilet and even a driver's sleeping quarters on a lower deck. Looking back through their window, they could see the old bus idling in the parking zone—a scene that faded in the dusk. Many of the passengers did not seem to realize fully that they were free. Silent apprehension was their riding companion.

The glare of floodlights startled them as the Mercedes coach came to a halt at the customs control station. Hans studied the detachment of armed troops on the East German side. He saw the massive concrete blocks along the road, the meshed wire, the posted danger signs warning of mines buried in the soil near the high-wire fences on both sides of the road. While stopped at the GDR control station, the East German plainclothesman presented to a GDR soldier a document attached to a copy of the bus's manifest. The soldier made a perfunctory pass down the aisle, turned, and left. Looking forward through the giant windshield, the twelve noticed an absence of wire and barbed wire and hidden-mine warning signs at the West German control station. When the coach slowed, approaching the West control station, an officer simply waved the driver on through the gate without having to stop. Once in the Federal Republic, Hans, Karl, and the others noticed immediately how smooth the highway pavement became and how quiet the ride. When they began to see road signs indicating directions and distance to such places as Kassel, Würzburg, and Frankfurt, the dramatic moment of awakening had come. Suddenly chatter and laughter rippled through the bus. The atmosphere had become much lighter and more relaxed.

"Karl, we're free! *We're free!*" Hans' excitement was uninhibited as usual. The experience of freedom and free expression of it was too new a thing. He didn't quite know what to do with it. But it sure felt good!

Karl only nodded, too overcome by emotion to speak.

They sat in silence for a little while. There were flashbacks. Karl pictured his brother, Albert, teasing him by snatching something off the shelf of the family store that Karl had carefully arranged and running zigzag through the store aisles and out into the street until Karl finally caught him. Hans could almost smell the new-mown hay on the farm of youthful days. Karl remembered the ridicule of a college classmate committed to Marxism over Karl possessing a picture postcard of San Francisco because it was implicit acceptance of capitalistic propaganda. Hans wondered about his lost love, Marie. Karl thought about his friend Fritz and whether or not they might resume their relationship one day. Being thrust into the unknown and uncertain future, they found a measure of comfort and security living in the past. After all, it can't be changed.

"Karl, what's the first thing you plan to do when we arrive?"

"I'll send a telegram to my parents and to Marlo."

"That's exactly what I'm going to do—send word to my father. 'I made it to the other side, and I'm all right.'"

The gentle vibration of the luxury coach relaxed them enough to drop off to sleep for a time until they reached the city limits of Giessen. They were jolted out of slumber by the coach tires striking the uneven railroad tracks traversing the highway.

Hans opened one eye and peered out the window. He had to squint to read the road sign illuminated by the headlights in the darkness—Gießen. Hans' blurred vision caught something blue, red, and white painted on the side of a large building along the side of the road. A line of floodlights gave the object color and shape in the darkness. Then it came into focus: the symbol of the American flag! He and his busload of companions were evidently passing an American military installation of some kind.

A sentinel for the free world, Hans thought.

They moved on toward the center of the city, winding past Berliner Platz on the right with its striking mosaic stone offering its own kind of joyous welcome to these unheralded refugees. Some three kilometers out from the city center, the coach made an arc around the train station. A dream had come true at last. How incredible it seemed in view of what had transpired over the last year.

Squealing brakes interrupted Karl's thoughts. Stepping onto West German soil was an irrefutable confirmation of freedom! It was Saturday, May 31, 1969. Karl and Hans would never forget this date, nor was it likely any of the others on board would forget.

The busload of passengers stood before a cluster of buildings that served as a refugee relocation center. With childlike awe and restrained joy, they inched toward the building, breathing an invigorating tonic of the chill night air.

Inside was a drone of excitement among other recent arrivals—some three busloads that week. Several groans were audible from a corner of the main lounge, where a number of individuals were huddled around a television set. Karl and Hans stepped closer to the animated group. A Frankfurt newscaster was reporting that Dr. Gustav Husak, the Communist Party leader of Czechoslovakia, had announced a purge of what he termed opportunistic elements. Husak was quoted as saying, "We cannot tolerate any anti-Soviet attitudes in our ranks." Husak had succeeded Alexander Dubček and the short-lived democratic experiment six weeks earlier.

"Husak is choking the last breath of freedom out of the Czechs!" someone in the group protested.

Hans winced, and his eyes darted about the room. He was not yet accustomed to such open expression of opinion, especially criticism of the Communist Eastern bloc.

Like the other new arrivals, Karl Mann was processed through an orientation procedure. The clerk assured him that he would be given complete information about admission to medical schools. Since Karl was unable to provide transcripts from Humboldt, he would have to take a series of college exams to determine his aptitude and level of academic acumen. Like the others, Karl was given a small ration of money for incidental expenses. Donations had been raised by the churches of West Germany. Karl and Hans were pleased to share a room at the center, for their friendship had blossomed over the last five months. Neither of them could get to sleep this night. They were simply too wound up with excitement and too full of new impressions to sort out. They spent much of the night recalling step-by-step their past experiences together as if they really needed to convince themselves that what was happening was real. Out of sheer exhaustion from their conversation, they nodded off to sleep at three o'clock. By that hour, the entire dormitory had quieted down.

Sunday was a day for relaxing at the refugee center or strolling down the avenue. It was a day for reminiscing privately in one's own inner sanctum. Karl and Hans walked downtown, quietly absorbed in their own respective thoughts. This was uncharacteristic of Hans because, by nature, he was so verbally expressive. But there was a whole lot to process mentally as well as emotionally.

They walked by the Goethe School in the vicinity of the Giessen train station. Karl motioned to Hans to go on. Karl wanted to sit on a bench near the school yard for a while. He was feeling melancholic.

He thought about Walter, of his boyhood school days, who had been expelled. And at a school flag ceremony, there was Erich, who had been overheard by the principal calling a National People's Army uniformed detachment stupid. Erich suffered the same fate as Walter. *Maybe Peter was the lucky one of the lot. He hanged himself! Peter saved himself from suffering indignities sure to be heaped upon him. No future career. Really sad.* Karl remembered that sympathetic students wore black armbands but were reprimanded. So the students removed their armbands. The pupils were not permitted to attend the funeral. That day, the school was patrolled, and school doors were locked. Nobody was allowed to talk openly about Peter. Karl had forgotten about most of that incident until this moment. He was in touch with some unfinished grief about the tragedy. *Oh yes, the young lad I met in prison—Richard. Ah, but there's nothing I can do about it now, only hope that Walter and Erich and my other school friends like them and Richard find peace for their souls in living as Peter has found in dying.*

Karl and Hans met up with each other hours later in their refugee center room.

"Hans, what did you do after we separated?"

"I went to the post office and sent a telegram to my father and brothers. I told them where I am. And you?"

"I just took time to think things through. I'll contact my family and Marlo tomorrow. I walked through the downtown, looking in shop windows. I was especially interested in a market and the variety of foods stocked on the shelves. Hans, I saw commodities I've seldom seen in our

GDR markets, even in our family market—many more fresh fruits and vegetables, good-quality sundries like toothpaste and toilet paper that we can't buy in East Germany. Then I visited a pharmacy that was open today! You wouldn't believe how well stocked it is with medicines of every kind! I was absolutely astonished! Well, tomorrow is going to be a very busy day. Good night, Hans."

"Good night, Karl."

CHAPTER 34

Monday morning proved to be as demanding as the first day of registration for classes at a university. First came the physical examination immediately following a seven o'clock breakfast call. Then each refugee was scheduled for a conference with a counselor. The routine began with filling out a voluminous form on personal and family history, including educational background and work experience.

"Why did you leave the German Democratic Republic" the counselor asked Karl.

"For the reason I stated on that form. I am engaged to be married to an American woman."

"Why did you not have her join you in East Germany?"

Even though the counselor represented a friendly nation and had a sincere, legitimate reason for asking that question, Karl was tired of the same questions with which he had been interrogated so many times before. He was reluctant to get into political issues. He really didn't wish to sound like an enemy of the GDR. He simply explained that Marlo would have no promising future living in East Germany given the current political climate.

"So I chose to leave, thinking I could continue my medical career and fulfill our wish to be married. I wanted more freedom to move about. It's as simple as that."

"Mr. Mann, you mention on this form that you have completed some of your academic work at Humboldt University. However, you do not have any transcripts in your file."

"I would have raised suspicion had I asked the dean for transcripts."

"Before we can consider placing you in a medical school in this country, we will need to have verification of your completed course work to date."

"What does that involve?"

"You will have to write and ask Humboldt to send you the information."

"But do you believe they will honor my request since I will show a West German address?"

"It is difficult to say. The GDR has proven to be inconsistent about such things."

"The orientation counselor I spoke with when I arrived here said that it would be possible for me to take a general examination on medical knowledge in lieu of transcripts."

"Yes, that is possible, of course. It is an arduous process, however. I don't recommend that except as a last resort."

"Well, then, what do you suggest I do?"

"Mr. Mann, perhaps you can enclose a letter of request with correspondence to your family in Meissen. They in turn can forward your request to Berlin, obtain your transcripts, and mail them to you."

"That may take some time."

"I realize that, but certainly not as much time as it took you to get to the Federal Republic of Germany!"

"That's true."

"Your options are to take the comprehensive examination or enroll in medical school as a first-year student and start over."

"No no no!"

"Then I suggest you get started writing that letter and posting it today. I will give you one of our official introductory forms to take with you to the university when you apply for admission. When you get your transcripts, attach them to these forms and submit them with your admission application. Our papers will place you in a higher level of priority for enrollment consideration."

"Thank you. How long am I able to stay here at the center?"

"As long as it takes you to get settled somewhere and find work or get enrolled in school. But space is limited. We expect more refugees in the weeks ahead. We hope you will be ready to leave here within a week."

"I have very little money, only what we received at orientation. You know, I had to forfeit my remaining East German marks before leaving the GDR."

"I understand your problem, believe me. Many East Germans being processed here face the same dilemma. There is a Church Charity Fund administered here to help you with a modest amount for food, transportation, and lodging. Go to the next office down the hall to apply for funds."

Karl secured enough to buy a train ticket to Stuttgart, where he might get temporary help from family friends. He and Hans completed their processing at the relocation center and took another walk downtown. They stopped at the post office long enough for Karl to send a telegram to his parents and Marlo. He included a request of his parents to send for his Humboldt transcripts.

The two men were filled with an indescribable sense of tranquility, euphoria, wholeness—something they had gone through hell to achieve. They did not take their victory lightly, but they did feel ready to celebrate.

As they crossed a street, Karl stopped abruptly. Hans looked on quizzically. Karl began to laugh, pointing to a bin of carrots at a nearby market.

"Hans, did I ever tell you about the old man and his bag of—"

"Yes, yes, Karl, you told me." He smiled and shook his head.

"I'll never be able to eat another carrot again without thinking of that poor old soul."

"And I may never eat another carrot!" replied Hans with a twinkle in his eye. He gave Karl a playful shove.

They walked a little farther and discovered a quaint restaurant. The interior was the inside of a giant old wine vat that had expelled its sweet red fluid decades ago, perhaps even a century ago. They decided this was a good time and place for a meal to celebrate their freedom. Neither could remember the last time they had eaten in a fine restaurant—or any kind of restaurant, for that matter. And then Karl nodded, and in a solemn whisper said, "Oh, I'm remembering Unter den Linden."

Hans's eyebrows shot up as he nodded his head and confessed, "I remember my 'last supper' in Koper, Yugoslavia, where I was only steps away from jumping over the line into Italy and liberty." They found a table at the far corner of a small dining room that reminded Hans of the setting in which he first encountered Marie in a Dresden café seemingly so long ago. The hurt of their separation had long since faded. Hans was now content to consign Marie to the past.

"What are your plans about school, Karl?"

"You know about the transcript situation. When I can, I'll apply for admission to Heidelberg and Tübingen."

"And Marlo?"

"Well, we had made plans . . ." Karl became tearful and turned his head aside for a minute.

Hans understood what Karl was feeling and simply waited patiently without a word.

Karl regained his composure. "Ah, we had planned, you know, to study together. She was planning to return and meet me here in West Germany." Karl paused to work on dissolving a hard lump in his throat. "In the meantime, she has completed her education. I suppose she can find a job while I finish medical school. It's been weeks since I last heard from her through my mother's letter to me at Cottbus."

"She still cares about you?"

"Yes, well, I hope she still loves me." Karl's eyes became moist again.

Hans grasped Karl's hand to convey reassurance. Words were inadequate. Words were cheap. Hans remained silent. The touch of a hand seemed enough.

Karl looked away again, wiped his face, and asked, "Tell me about your plans."

"I'll be leaving in a few days to stay with my relatives up north in Bremerhaven, my uncle and aunt. He's a brother of my mother."

"What about work?"

"I don't know yet. My uncle is an engineer. Maybe he will have some contacts for me that will lead to a job. He lives in quite an industrial area. So that will be to my advantage. But you know, my specialty is food production. My dream is to become an agricultural consultant."

"Hans, do you think Marlo will come back?"

Hans studied thoughtfully the look on Karl's face. He knew he had to answer his friend's question. "Yes, Karl, I believe she will come back to you."

"All of this was for her, you know. I left my family, friends, home, university . . . those awful dogs, the humiliating trial, prison . . . all of that for Marlo! This is Germany, yes, but this is a strange land too. Do you know what I mean?"

Hans nodded. "Listen, Karl, I *know* she will come. But even if Marlo doesn't return for whatever reason, this can be a new life for you here. There is a freedom here we have never known before. It will be good for you, for us!"

Karl sat in silence, pondering what his friend had just said. His eyes looked deeply into Hans's eyes with an acknowledgment of the truth of Hans's observation. "Thank you, my friend."

Hans returned a smile.

They studied the menu, mindful of their scant resources. So many things looked good!

The waitress approached their table. "You may order anything you wish, gentlemen."

They reacted with surprise.

"Compliments of the man at the table over there."

Karl and Hans turned around to thank the stranger just as he arose to leave.

"Sir, thank—" they began to say in unison.

"No need to say anything. This is just a way to say welcome to the Federal Republic of Germany, welcome to your new home!" he shouted as he went out the door.

Karl and Hans stared at the waitress in disbelief.

"He comes in here regularly. He will pay your bill," she assured them.

"Who is he?" asked Hans

"I don't know his name," she replied, "but he is a wealthy businessman in Giessen. That's all I know."

The two ordered the kind of superb German cuisine that institutional cooking they had endured, German notwithstanding, was incapable of producing.

"Hans, be sure to save our wedding date. I want you to be my best man!"

"I would be honored! I didn't hear you say the date."

"I didn't. But save it anyway!"

They laughed.

The waitress brought them two large steins of beer. They raised their steins in salute to each other and ceremoniously blew off the foam that crested the top of their containers.

"Think of it, Karl! This is the first beer we've had in a year or more. How does a German manage to survive that long without his beer?"

Karl joined Hans in laughter. Their new life was under way.

Chapter 35

At five fifteen, Marlo had just returned home from her teaching job at a local college. Esther was polishing the diningroom table. Wesley was on a business trip. Diane was reading a novel in her room. About that time, there came a knock on the door at the Farrell's residence. Esther opened the door.

"Western Union delivering a telegram for Marlo Farrell," the uniformed gentleman solemnly announced.

Marlo raced to the door. "I'm Marlo Farrell!" she exclaimed.

"Please sign here." He held out a clipboard on which was attached an official receipt form. Marlo hastily scribbled her signature. "Good day, ladies."

"Good-bye, and thank you!" Marlo replied with nervous excitement in her voice.

Closing the door, she stood motionless for several minutes, clutching the telegram. *Could this be the good news from Karl?* She turned the telegram over and over in her hands, smoothing the surfaces of the envelope while staring off in the distance.

Finally, her mother looked at her with arms folded. "Well, aren't you going to open it?"

Marlo opened the envelope to find a cryptic coded message in German from Kurt and Eva. She gave out a scream that would wake the dead! Esther looked on with a sense of shock. Diane bolted out of her room. "What is it?" she asked her sister. "Hurry up! I can't stand this."

"Karl is free! Karl is free!" Marlo trembled. Tears streamed down her face. Marlo, Esther, and Diane embraced with shouts of joy.

When she calmed down, Marlo decided to place a phone call to friends of the Mann family living in Stuttgart. Perhaps they would have details of Karl's whereabouts.

"Hello! Hello!" she said as she sought to find the correct words in German to ask her questions. There was a long delay characteristic of transatlantic communications in the 1960s. She wondered if she was being heard. She began to speak again as the person in Germany was also speaking. She was listening to the unintelligible voice of someone in a stupor. There was a click. The transmission ceased.

"Oh my gosh!" Marlo groaned. "I forgot the time difference. In Germany it's the middle of the night. I woke up the person who answered the phone."

A while later another telegram was delivered. It was from Karl. Marlo held it close to her face and kissed it. She looked at the transmission date—2 *Juni* 1969. "It was sent this morning!" Marlo cried out. "He says he's at a Giessen refugee center in West Germany, and will get back in touch later when his plans are firm."

"Imagine the telegram from *East* Germany arriving here first!" Esther exclaimed incredulously. "I'd like to call your father right now," she added, "but he's on a road trip for several days. "We'll have to wait for him to call this evening."

Soon after, when Wesley checked in by phone, Marlo told her father the good news.

Marlo's heart was racing. She had difficulty sleeping that night. It was a challenge to concentrate at work the remainder of the week. Marlo was so emotionally drained that she decided to take some vacation time from teaching summer session. Word spread like wildfire to relatives and friends everywhere. For days, every knock at the door, every ring of the telephone caused a frenzy. *Could it be?* . . . *No, it wasn't.* **This time**, *could it be?* . . . *No, it wasn't.*

Two weeks passed before Marlo heard from Karl again. This time he wrote a long letter. She waited until everyone was home for dinner to share the contents.

"Karl writes that he has been staying with family friends in Stuttgart. He received his transcripts from Humboldt, and his admission application has been accepted at Heidelberg University Medical School. He expects to move to an apartment near the university by July first. The school dean told him he has enough credits to be able to complete his basic studies by next summer! Then he will do his internship and declare a branch of medicine to specialize in—another four years."

"That's wonderful news!" said her father.

Diane clapped her hands gleefully, and her mother gave out her typical shriek of joy.

"There's more," Marlo continued with a wrinkled brow. "Well, Karl wants me to come to Heidelberg and live there while he finishes school—"

"In his apartment?" Esther asked with pursed lips.

"Now, Mother! He thinks it would be good for us to have a year to test our relationship before we get married. I agree. And, **no**, he can't have me stay at his apartment. He says university policy does not allow for what they call student cohabitation."

Esther and Wesley both exhaled a long breath. Diane simply rolled her eyes.

"He needs to know what my decision will be. I do want to go. I've saved up enough money to pay for my flight. I can stay at a youth hostel until I find a job. The hostels are very cheap."

"Well, my dear, I can see you have your heart set on this plan," said Wesley. "We can help you with expenses until you get settled with a good job. Perhaps you can find an apartment near the campus."

"Oh, thank you for your understanding! I love you all so much." They all exchanged kisses and hugs and tears of joy.

On June 24, Marlo sent a letter to Karl. She stated she would book a flight from San Francisco to Frankfurt, arriving July 4. She picked that date as a fitting symbol of Karl's new independence from the oppressive government of East Germany.

Once the arrangements were made, Wesley reflected on the experiences of Marlo and Karl over the last year and a half. When he and Esther had gone to bed, he shared his thoughts with his wife. "You know, this total experience of the two has certainly strengthened their character. Just imagine the valuable lessons about life they have already mastered. To my way of thinking, it all seems to reinforce the notion that nothing of value in God's creation is ever lost, that some good is salvaged from the worst of circumstances. What do you think, Esther?"

She nodded with a smile. "I think I hear a sermon in the making." She poked him, gave him a peck on the cheek, and turned out the light. "Good night."

"Yes, it *is* a good night!"

CHAPTER 36

Karl was counting the days remaining until Marlo's arrival. He quickly fell in love with the charm of Heidelberg, that old city spread along the banks of the Neckar River.

When Marlo arrived, Karl took her on a sightseeing tour of the city. Only after three days at a student hostel, Marlo was accepted for a secretarial job with the American Sixth Army stationed near Heidelberg. Karl helped her find a cozy apartment nearer to her work than to Karl's place on campus.

Karl found medical school exceedingly demanding, just as his counselor at Karl-Marx-Stadt had warned. His striving for excellence, his pushing to prove himself as a former East German, meant that he and Marlo had little time to themselves—Saturday night dinner and a few hours on Sunday. They turned lean quantity time into quality time, sharing their hopes, dreams, and fears about the unknown future. They compared notes on what they enjoyed doing with their leisure time and were pleasantly surprised that they both enjoyed music, art museums, reading, and tent camping. They explored their likes and dislikes about sex. That was not a topic discussed at home during Marlo's growing-up years. She was a bit embarrassed about that discussion. They talked about how they handle money—both of them tending toward frugality. Karl was surprised to discover that Marlo enjoyed playing the stock market.

"How did you get interested in that?" Karl asked.

"I had a college friend who showed me how she did day-trading. It paid off for her. She made enough money to cover the cost of textbooks. And my brother-in-law Lee taught me a good deal about stock market investing. For me, it's a hobby."

Karl was amazed.

There ensued a lengthy discussion about where they would live after finishing school and following the wedding—Germany or the United States. And they talked about how many children they would want to have. If an argument ended in the middle of a sentence on one weekend, that sentence would resume the following weekend. Both of them valued careful planning for the future on anything they undertook. This predisposed them for some rather intense, protracted discussions about what each wanted in a marriage relationship.

The budding of new life in the spring of 1970 brought the onslaught of written and oral exams. But Marlo's preoccupation was the need to plan for the wedding.

"Marlo, I need to concentrate on my exams. I'm feeling a bit overwhelmed."

"I realize that. But can't we at least talk about a place and a date?"

"I suppose," he said with resignation.

"So when? Late this summer?"

"Maybe a little later. September?"

"Okay. Where?"

"I know you want your family to be present. It is highly unlikely that my family would be permitted to come out of the GDR even for a wedding. The government has been known to deny an exit visa for some members of a household as a way of motivating the one permitted to leave to return home. If that were to be a requirement for the Mann family, I know that my father would not leave without my mother and my mother would not leave without my father. Albert would have no chance of getting a visa on his own. I suppose my grandparents can leave the GDR simply because of their advanced age. In fact, the government would be just as pleased to have them leave and not return. Then the government would not have to pay their pensions."

Marlo looked on with astonishment. "Is that the way it really is? I mean, elderly people being able to leave but forfeiting their retirement pay?"

"Yes, that's true. But when they leave the GDR, they leave behind any property they cannot carry out with them—land, homes, furnishings. If they are lucky, they will have relatives with whom they can leave their property. So all of this is to say there is nothing to hold us in Germany for the wedding."

"Let's get married in the United States."

"Yes, I would like that."

She pulled Karl close with a big hug, burying his face in her ample bosom. "Oh, Karl, you're wonderful!"

Karl did not rush to extricate himself from the headlock. His nose welcomed the fragrance of her perfume wafting upward with her body warmth from her cleavage. His amorous thoughts easily turned to more intimate delights. But Marlo pushed him upright.

"So what do you have in mind?" she asked, knowing full well what he had in mind at *that* moment. "About being married in the United States, that is!"

Karl smiled sheepishly. "Well, I mean, at least your family will be able to attend. No matter where the wedding takes place, we're certain my family can't attend."

Marlo kissed him on the neck.

"Where in the United States? *San Francisco* maybe?" The magic of those two words spelling the city by the bay elicited a broad smile on Karl's face.

"I hate to disappoint you, but maybe not San Francisco. There is a city near San Francisco that would be perfect though. Berkeley is across the bay from San Francisco. You'll like Berkeley. It's a university town like Heidelberg. There's a church in Berkeley I really like, and it has a wonderful organ. Besides, my brother-in-law is the minister there. My parents live near Berkeley. It is a convenient location for all my family members."

"Okay, that sounds good."

Their decision was sealed with a kiss—a long, passionate kiss.

Marlo pushed Karl back again and gasped for air. "Karl, I think sometime on the weekend of September fifth or sixth will be good." Marlo flipped the pages of a nearby wall calendar to check weekend dates. "That is a holiday weekend in America. We call it Labor Day weekend. The following Monday is a national holiday. My sister Linda and her family will find it easier to make the trip from their home in Phoenix, Arizona. That's quite a distance away."

"Ah, September fifth will be an easy date to remember—"

"Oh yes, that's your father's birthday. Since your family can't attend the wedding, that will be a nice way to honor them."

"So we will be married in Berkeley on September the fifth. Good!"

The final decision was sealed with another lingering kiss. Karl caressed every contour of her body.

"Karl! This is *not* your human anatomy lab, you know!" The spell was broken.

Meanwhile, Hans had moved to Bonn. The West German government was impressed with his credentials and decided to put his expertise to work on behalf of the government. He was offered a position with the foreign diplomatic corps, being groomed for a team that would travel to underdeveloped countries. Their task would be to consult with indigenous technicians about irrigation installations and other matters to enhance food production and the quality of their inhabitants' lives. The task fit Hans's idealism perfectly.

In response to Karl's newsy letter about marriage plans, Hans paid a visit to his friend in Heidelberg. He and Marlo met for the first time. Hans was impressed with her graciousness and tenacity.

"Hans, do you remember the time I asked you to save the wedding date?"

"Yes, and I circled every date on this year's calendar!" That elicited a chuckle from all three.

"Well, I hope that includes September the fifth!" quipped Karl.

"It does. I will speak to my supervisor about delaying my overseas assignment."

"We'll send you information about the time and location of the wedding in Berkeley, California," Marlo assured Hans. "And we'll send you a list of places near the church where you can stay. I'm sure we can find someone in the family to shuttle you from and to the airport."

"Thank you! I look forward to seeing you in America in a month or so. Tschüss!"

"Auf Wiedersehen!"

Midsummer forced Karl into around-the-clock preparations for his medical exams. The elder Manns in Meissen invited Marlo to spend several weeks with them and take care of wedding details. The border crossing was surprisingly easy. In the quiet family home above the store, Marlo wrote letters to her family concerning local wedding arrangements at the Berkeley church and the role each of her four sisters were to play in the ceremony. She asked her father and Doreen's minister husband, Dick, to perform the ceremony and asked Janice's husband, John Emory, also a member of the clergy, to serve as second best man. She thought John's modest command of German would be useful to both her groom and Hans, neither of whom spoke or understand much English. Marlo also requested that Linda be her matron of honor and Diane serve as a bridesmaid. With their beautiful singing voices, Doreen and Janice were to share their talent at the wedding.

Eva and Marlo traveled to Dresden where the bride-to-be was fitted for a gown.

"Marlo, my dear, this pattern will be lovely on you." Eva pointed to an empress-style gown embellished with a special Plauen lace.

"I love it!" Marlo said. She nodded approval to the dressmaker. Marlo picked out a black-and-brown checked wool-blend dress for her going-away outfit after the wedding.

The Manns hosted a bridal shower for Marlo. A few relatives and close friends of the Mann family gathered. Even the modest number of gifts given to the couple presented a formidable challenge for Marlo to transport them to Heidelberg. The solution: Karl's maternal grandfather, a widowed octogenarian, agreed to accompany Marlo back to Heidelberg with the gifts. He had made a number of trips each year to relatives in West Germany and was reasonably certain of getting a travel visa for this occasion. He succeeded.

Marlo and the elder Martin Schneider boarded a train for the border. Schneider carried the large clothing box containing the wedding gown. Marlo balanced in her grip the packaged dress, a vacuum cleaner, a mixer, and a box of everyday dishware. Unable to have a free hand with which to grab a handrail and unable to see her feet, Marlo carefully felt her way up and down the stairs. She was mindful of the fact that West German trains would not remain at the border station at her pleasure. On both sides of the border, they had to detach themselves from their parcels for inspection and to display their passports and visas. When they finally got to their seats on the Federal Republic train, Marlo sank into the comfortable chair and vowed not to move one muscle until they got to Heidelberg.

When Marlo and Martin Schneider arrived in Heidelberg, Karl arranged to put them up in his apartment for the remaining week of Karl's exams. Marlo slept in Karl's bed while Martin Schneider curled up on the sofa. On those rare occasions when Karl caught a few winks in the midst of study in the library's stacks and taking incremental exams, he would either flop on the floor near his desk, wrapped up like a mummy in a quilt, or snuggle up against Marlo on the narrow bed.

His tireless efforts paid off. He got word that he not only passed his comprehensive written and oral exams but also finished near the top of his class! Marlo and Karl were alone in his apartment when Karl received the notice and was reading the results. Marlo was giving him a back massage, unlocking tense muscles around his shoulders and neck.

"Oh, Marlo! This is more than I could have ever hoped for." He drew a deep breath and slowly exhaled.

"I'm so proud of you! I'm not surprised you did so well."

After they accompanied Martin to the train station for his trip back to Meissen, Karl and Marlo began packing for their adventure in the United States. Though they were filled with excitement about the wedding and their new life together, they felt some pathos about leaving Germany, which played such a significant part in how their magical meeting and romance began. However, they knew that one day they would return.

CHAPTER 37

Saturday, September 5, 1970, was a newsworthy date for such an occasion as a Berkeley wedding, for which the rest of the world did not come to a screeching halt. Middle East peace talks stalled when Israel announced intentions of a boycott until Egypt withdrew Soviet missiles alleged to have been transported into the Suez Canal. Greek guerrillas hijacked four jetliners bound for New York with 619 passengers' lives at stake. California congressman Don Edwards lashed out against the economic policies of the Nixon administration that allowed a 6 percent inflation rate to persist over the preceding twelve-month period. The nation was spending a half a million dollars to kill one Vietcong. Ralph Nader charged that General Motors lied to Congress to cover up alleged safety hazards of the Convair automobile. California governor Ronald Reagan began his fall reelection campaign against Democratic challenger Jesse Unruh. Football legend Vince Lombardi died. Oakland A's Jim "Catfish" Hunter pitched his first no-hitter of the season Friday night, beating the Kansas City Royals five to nothing at the Oakland Coliseum. At nearby Berkeley, Telegraph Avenue continued to be a people-watchers' paradise with all manner of university student fads on parade up and down the crowded thoroughfare. The Hari Krishnas were chanting to drumbeats on a street corner while vendors were hawking their wares at curbside. In the eighty-degree summer heat, the press of humanity along Telegraph exuded a heavy layer of incense mixed with body odors and marijuana.

Within a few blocks of Telegraph and University of California's notorious Sather Gate, hallowed ground for student protests, was cathedral-like Trinity United Methodist Church, which Marlo's family had reserved for the wedding. Late in August, Karl and Marlo arrived in California. Hans flew into New York City and took a bus to the West Coast. John Emory had the task of meeting Hans at the bus terminal and escorting him for the remainder of his stay. Karl and Hans had an opportunity to meet Marlo's family and see the sights of the Bay Area, including San Francisco and Muir Woods. Of course, Karl was especially gratified to visit San Francisco. Linda and Lee arrived from Arizona. The entire family, along with Karl and Hans, enjoyed German cuisine at Beethoven's Restaurant.

"This city is as charming as I had heard about and seen in photos," he said. "If I cannot live in Germany, I would live here!"

On the afternoon of September 5, several hundred wedding guests poured into Trinity Church. The only one to arrive late was a redheaded Irish lady, Esther Farrell. But to those who knew Esther, her tardiness was not a great surprise. Lee served as usher.

Karl and Hans nervously slipped into their rental attire as John helped them identify American garment sizes and, in his halting German, answer their questions about the logistics of the ceremony.

Doreen and Janice sang their songs. Doreen offered a solo, "Ich liebe dich"; Janice sang "Whither Thou Goest"; and the two offered a duet, "O Lord, Most Holy." The Emorys' two oldest daughters, Jody and Julie, started down the aisle to light the candelabra. They began their entrance, walking side by side. Then Jody started to lag a step behind her sister. Her lighted acolyte wick swung in the direction of Julie's hair. For a brief impish moment, Jody wondered about the excitement she might cause by setting Julie's hair on fire! A faint smile appeared on her face. But Jody quickly regained her proper position by Julie's side, and they approached the candelabra. All the while, Julie was oblivious to the aborted prank. Janice and John's youngest daughter, Jerilyn, fulfilled the role of flower girl, casting rose petals down the aisle with uncommon childlike aplomb. Linda and Diane displayed grace and poise. Marlo was escorted by her father, who then stood with Dick to conduct the ceremony. Marlo exuded a glow rarely seen on the face of brides. Her eyes sparkled. Karl was transfixed, in awe of her beauty. Throughout the ceremony, John translated the vows and cued his two charges on what to do next. Had the couple been high-profile celebrities, this extraordinary wedding would have made the front page of the newspaper's society page! It was remarkable enough that this wedding uniquely united East and West of global geopolitics.

The reception was grand. The women of the church provided a festive buffet and an elegant three-tiered wedding cake. Marlo and Karl stood for over an hour to greet wedding guests. Marlo was careful to introduce her relatives, including retired colonel John Stover, to her new husband. By this time in his life, John's legs were weak. He shuffled his steps slowly with the aid of a walker.

"It might interest you to know that Karl's father was a German soldier during World War II," Marlo informed her uncle.

With a faint smile, Stover gave Karl a firm handshake. He thought, *Hmm, turn the calendar back and we'd be mortal enemies! I wonder where his father was deployed.*

CHAPTER 38

And then came the honeymoon—as incredibly strange as any honeymoon could possibly be! It was of the kind you only hear about in jokes or see on the movie screen created out of the wild imagination of a screenwriter!

The Reverend Dr. Farrell had been asked by a national church agency to conduct a study through interviews across the United States. He thought it would be cost-effective to combine his cross-country research project with a honeymoon that would provide an expansive sightseeing opportunity especially for Karl. He felt as though he could serve as a tour guide of sorts. As plans progressed, it was decided that the newlyweds would *enjoy* the company of both Wesley and Esther as well as Diane and Hans! If ever there was a test of endurance of a marriage just under way, this had to be it!

Marlo didn't say anything but only looked out of the corner of her eye at Karl. He appeared to politely accede to the plan. Hans thought of it as a grand adventure. Diane wasn't quite sure what to think but preferred being a sojourner to staying home alone.

All six plus a mountain of luggage piled into a rented Volkswagen bus and started the trans-American "honeymoon" at the California coastal resort town of Santa Cruz. Along the journey, Hans elected to sleep in the van to help reduce expenses while the elder Farrells, Diane, and the honeymooners stayed in their respective motel rooms. Each morning, Hans kept watch for departing room guests. Before a housekeeper could get to a vacated room, Hans slipped in to take a shower and emerged refreshed for the next leg of the journey—a variation on a theme of survival for a once-upon-a-time escape artist! When the Farrells eventually caught on to Hans's early morning escapade, they chose to make their room, shower, and a towel available to him. Somewhere between the West Coast and the Continental Divide in the Rockies, there was a blissful, exotic night when the honeymooners' marriage was finally consummated.

Several weeks passed as Marlo and Karl got comfortable with the routine and did enjoy seeing the sights of national parks and other delights. Wesley Farrell did his best to schedule research interviews with local clergy in close proximity to scenic venues. The plan seemed to be working far better than initially anticipated by Marlo, Karl, or any impartial observers.

When the sojourners reached the East Coast, Farrell arrived at the home of a Massachusetts family who were community and church leaders where Janice and John lived in the early 1960s while John completed graduate school at Boston University School of Theology. Wesley had sent a letter to the Fulkersons, requesting a visit and an interview.

The timing was perfect. Autumn colors splashed across the landscape of the town of Bernardston only a few miles from the Vermont and New Hampshire borders.

"Hello! Floyd Fulkerson?" inquired Wesley.

"Yes, but folks call me Bud. You can call me Bud too."

Wesley introduced himself and the purpose of the visit, referring to the letter he had sent.

"Oh, Janice Emory is your daughter and John your son-in-law! Oh yes, we remember them well and have kept in touch over the years. We are so happy to meet you! Please come in," insisted Bud. He and his wife, Jane, were accustomed to hosting almost anyone who appeared at their front door. They were known for their generous hospitality. "We are preparing to leave today to spend the weekend at our lakeside house in New Hampshire. Please come along and join us. We can have our visit there."

"We don't want to be an impos—"

"Not at all," responded Jane. "Besides, we have lots of space for overnight houseguests at the lake. It's a short drive from here."

"We're lucky to have such nice weather, almost like summer," added Bud.

The VW bus followed the Fulkersons up the road to the lake. The warm sun was inviting for hours at the shore.

"Does anyone want to water-ski?" asked Bud. He and Jane owned a boat with an inboard motor and water ski equipment. They and their adult children were avid water-skiers.

Everyone declined except Marlo. She was eager for a new experience. She seemed to forget that she wasn't a particularly good swimmer. At the insistence of the Fulkersons, Marlo was fitted with a life jacket. Nervous about her offer, Marlo chose first to ride in the boat while someone else skied. Jane said she would demonstrate. After one pass around the lake, Jane made a beach landing to the thrill of onlookers. Then, Bud showed Marlo how to steer and set the speed of the boat. He gave her a chance to give it a try. As Marlo brought the boat close to the dock, she mistakingly sped up instead of cutting the throttle. The boat hit and bounced off the dock pillar. With a red face and without a prior thought, Marlo shouted, "Lolo did it!" Esther heard Marlo say that and broke into uncontrollable laughter. When she regained her composure, she told everyone the story about Lolo.

"When Marlo was about five years old," Esther began, "she had an imaginary friend she named Lolo. Whenever Marlo misbehaved, she would blame it on Lolo. 'Lolo did it!' she would contend. After a while, Marlo stopped mentioning Lolo. I asked her one day what happened to Lolo that she never mentioned her name anymore. Marlo replied, 'She went to hell!'" Everyone convulsed with laughter.

This time Bud sat at the wheel and throttle. Marlo positioned herself behind the boat on the skis, hanging on to the grip bar tethered to the boat. She tried again and again until finally she managed to hang on to the grip, keep her center of gravity slightly back with knees bent, and point her ski tips up out of the water. Marlo was launched and stayed afloat for perhaps thirty seconds. Everyone else had lined up at the lake's edge to cheer her on. Her father marveled at Marlo's persistence—something he had never witnessed before. It confirmed what he had heard about Marlo's determined effort to get to Meissen the Christmas of 1967.

At the close of the weekend, the sojourners expressed their gratitude to the Fulkersons for such a wonderful visit and went on their way. On Monday, the letter to which Wesley referred that had been mailed to the Fulkersons was delivered to their mailbox. Years later, with chagrin, the Farrells learned about it. "Bud never showed any sign of surprise at our arrival!" Wesley exclaimed. Wesley concluded his research project with interviews in Washington DC and New York City, which gave his passengers an opportunity to visit historic sites. In New York, Hans, Karl, and Marlo caught their flights to Germany. Wesley, Esther, and Diane returned home via famed Route 66.

Hans was tasked by the West German government to offer his consulting services in Third World countries. He went to the Cameroon, a onetime German colony in central West Africa, to teach farmers how to grow peanuts as a good source of protein. After a few years, he married and became the father of two daughters.

Karl resumed his academics at Heidelberg University, completing his internship in June 1974. The following year he finished his doctoral dissertation and was awarded *magna cum laude*. He declared oncology as his area of specialization. Karl was given an opportunity to return to the United States to observe various treatment programs at a clinic in San Jose, California. Marlo was delighted to travel with him and arranged time to visit her family.

Then it was back to Heidelberg, where Karl spent four months interning at the university's Institute of Pathology. His researches led to findings that brought him lecture invitations in Vienna, Lyon, and York in 1975 and 1976. Much of his work was published in medical journals. Having passed the rigorous English medical examination for foreign graduates in July of 1976, he had an opportunity to return to America with Marlo. Because of his marriage to Marlo, he was granted a US immigration visa as a permanent resident. In 1977, he worked as a clinical director, monitoring hypertension detection with follow-up programs—a project of the National Heart and Lung Institute. It was the summer of 1977 that Marlo gave birth to their first child, a daughter named Greta. Over the years, Greta evidenced her mother's musical talent at the keyboard and her father's aptitude for medical science. She has pursued a career in obstetrics and gynecology. There followed the birth of a son, Rainer, who showed promise in architecture and then a daughter, Margret, who would excel as a pharmacist. Marlo was pregnant with Margret while visiting family Stateside. Then a serious problem developed. The placenta was beginning to separate from the wall of the uterus. Marlo was ordered to total bed rest by a doctor in the Sacramento area, where Marlo was visiting a sister. Upon hearing the news, Karl rushed to her side from a speaking engagement halfway around the world. Several months later, she gave birth to Margret.

During the children's formative years, when Karl was in such demand as a worldwide lecturer regarding oncological research and patient treatment programs, Marlo was the nurturing parent for her children. She was tenderhearted and sympathetic. Greta, Rainer, and Margret knew they could tell her their troubles and she would listen with empathy. From their early age, Marlo taught them to be bilingual. They became proficient in English as well as in their native German. American family members were often amused and impressed when six-year-old Greta would shift back and forth between the two languages, depending upon with whom she was interacting.

Whether having piano students in her home, going downtown to shop, or attending church services on Sunday, Marlo was unpretentious. She seldom took time to apply makeup or get her hair permed. Her natural beauty required no assistance. Marlo found fulfillment musically, singing in the city's Lutheran church choir and the Mannheim Opera Company. In her spare time, she continued day-trading on the stock market. She remained a strong advocate for Amnesty International and would discover ways to send messages to families whose loved ones had been incarcerated for political reasons. Once, she prevailed upon her brother-in-law John Emory to mail letters of information to Russian families while he and Janice were traveling in the USSR. Marlo made frequent trips to the United States to spend time with family and relatives. Sorrow intruded upon their lives when Wesley Farrell suddenly died of a heart attack in the summer of 1980 at the age of seventy-five and later when Esther died of a heart ailment at the age of seventy-seven in December of 1986.

On the tenth anniversary of his prison release, Karl arranged for his parents, along with Albert and his new wife, Anita, to leave the GDR and make a new home for themselves near Heidelberg. They left many assets behind, but Kurt was able to sell the store and living quarters upstairs to a friend. In that year, Karl and Marlo took Kurt and Eva with them on a trip to America to visit family. The elder Manns joined Marlo, Karl, and the Emorys on a whale-watching boat excursion in Monterey Bay. Coming within fifty feet of the whales, Kurt and Eva were in awe of this new experience of watching the whales do their graceful sounding.

In spite of hardships and personal grief, these were good, productive years for the young Mann family. Kurt and Eva continued to live hearty lives well into their eighties.

EPILOGUE

Three months after 9/11, Greta and Rainer were pursuing their careers. Margret was a teenager, studying college preparatory courses at the gymnasium. Karl had a rare week at home without speaking engagements. His teaching load at the university was light. It was a time for Marlo, Margret, and him to make leisurely preparations for Christmas and plan their annual ski vacation in Switzerland.

Marlo complained of flu symptoms on December 9. Karl ordered her to bed and nursed her with plenty of liquids and chicken noodle soup. On the eleventh of December, as Karl was getting into bed, Marlo suddenly began to choke, gasp, and writhe uncontrollably. Karl was stunned by what he saw. He began to perform CPR and phoned paramedics, who arrived within minutes and began to apply standard interventions.

Margret was in shock. Karl did not want to leave her at the house or subject her to hospital emergency events. He called his parents to come to the house and stay with Margret.

"Marlo! Marlo!" Karl cried out. "Please wake up! We are helping you! Please, please, Marlo!" He felt so helpless, yet he was a doctor skilled at bringing patients back from the brink of death. *I should be able to help my wife! Why can't I revive her? What's wrong with me!*

The paramedics rushed her to a nearby hospital. Karl insisted on accompanying her. Efforts continued to be made to stabilize her. She was placed on a ventilator and taken to ICU. Totally exhausted, Karl kept a vigil at her side. He had phoned his brother. Albert arrived quickly to stay with Karl at Marlo's bedside.

A few hours passed well into the night. About 4:00 AM a hospital cardiologist came into the room. He looked into the blurry eyes of Karl. "Dr. Mann, I'm sorry. It doesn't look good. The electroencephalogram shows no brain activity." The doctor displayed the printout for Karl to peruse.

Karl studied it carefully for several minutes, shaking his head in dismay.

"I'll leave you for a few minutes while you think about next steps," the doctor said.

Karl looked at Albert, who really wanted to look away. "Albert, my head tells me there is no hope of resuscitating her." Karl stroked her forehead and cheeks with tenderness. "But my gut does not want to let her go." His eyes welled up with tears.

Albert did not say a word. He simply could not find any words to say. He reached out and hugged his brother around the neck and wept.

It seemed as though an eon passed during what were a mere ten minutes when the cardiologist returned with a nurse at his side.

Karl looked up, shaking his head. "Turn off that damn machine," he said with stark resignation.

"You sure?" the physician asked.

"Yes . . . yes . . . yes."

The cardiologist signaled the nurse to click off the ventilator. They all sat silent for several minutes. The cardiologist instructed the nurse to pronounce. She studied Marlo's pupils and checked for a pulse with her stethoscope. She placed a mirror to Marlo's nose and open mouth to look for the slightest hint of breath fogging the mirror's surface. All signs indicated death. As the nurse pronounced Marlo's passing in the early morning hours of December 12, 2001, Karl gently closed her eyelids and her mouth as he had done so many times before when his patients had passed. Karl and Albert sat at her side, absolutely horrified, unable to assimilate the reality of what had happened during the last few hours. Finally, Karl threw himself on Marlo with hugs and kisses and the spilling of tears. Albert rubbed his brother's shoulders and back and then gently drew Karl away from Marlo's corpse to settle into the chair.

A while later, Karl gained composure. He and Albert stepped out of the room, hesitating at the doorway for one last look in disbelief.

"She looks peaceful," Albert whispered.

"She looks like an angel, a beautiful a-a . . .," Karl barely managed to articulate.

With Albert at his side, Karl lumbered down the deserted hallway to a suite of medical offices. Karl found the hospital chief medical examiner just arriving for his daily rounds. Mystified by Marlo's death, Karl asked to have an autopsy performed. *I need to know . . . I need to know why she died.*

Though the clock read seven thirty, it was still dark across the landscape when Albert took Karl home. Karl sat numb, staring at a wall. Albert made the necessary phone calls to the immediate family, Karl's medical colleagues at the university, close friends, and the Lutheran pastor, who quickly came to the house to offer Karl spiritual and emotional support.

"God, she was only fifty-four," Karl mumbled to himself. "*Why* couldn't I save her!"

The following day, Greta contacted family members in the United States and reported that a funeral was being planned for December 19. Greta expressed the hope that as many as possible from the United States would be able to attend. Doreen, Linda, and John Emory made the decision to represent the American side of the family. For various reasons, others could not go.

The family's church was filled to standing room only on that nineteenth day of December. Karl huddled with Greta, Rainer, and Margret in the front row of seats. Resting before them on the steps to the altar was the closed coffin. Seated near the family were the elder Manns, Albert and Anita, Doreen, Linda, and John. Behind the altar sat the choir of forty voices. Out of respect for Marlo, one of their number, her choral chair was left empty with the exception of a bouquet of flowers resting upon it. The pastor spoke words of comfort and a summary of Marlo's life and achievements. The choir sang a poignant arrangement of Bach's "Jesu, Joy of Man's Desiring," accompanied by the pipe organ and an oboe.

Following the funeral, everyone in the family walked back to the house. Food was brought in by friends. Life experiences were remembered; stories were told with a mix of laughter and crying. It was a time for closure, the end of one chapter in a family's life with more chapters yet to be written.

Karl was puzzled why he had not heard from Hans Heinrich. It would be learned months later that Hans had been working in a remote village in India, where the message of Marlo's death did not reach him for several weeks.

The day before the funeral, the medical examiner had phoned Karl to report that the cause of death was thrombosis due to atherosclerosis. "Dr. Mann," he assured Karl, "there was absolutely nothing you could have done to save your wife. I'm sure you know that." Of course, Karl understood that, but it eased his mind to hear it from the medical examiner. The physician went on to say, "If, as you reported to me, your wife's parents died of heart disease, then you will want to advise her siblings to see a cardiologist for a checkup." Karl understood the urgency of that.

Overnight, Marlo's body was cremated in preparation for a private burial service. It was a chilly morning with a wintry breeze stirring. The family, including the three from the States, gathered in the cemetery chapel, which itself was dank. The plain container of ashes rested on the altar. The Lutheran pastor entered and offered some words and prayed. He lifted the container and led a quiet, solemn procession to the grave site in a beautiful garden-like section of the cemetery grounds. The sun was attempting to break through a layer of clouds. Everyone stood close together to keep warm.

The cleric lowered the box into the opened plot. He said a prayer and then, in deference to family sensitivities, gestured to John Emory to offer a committal prayer in English. Emotions and the bitter cold made it difficult for John to speak, but he offered his heartfelt prayer nonetheless.

Folks remained at the site for a few moments, wiping each other's tears and offering loving hugs. Eva and Kurt had reserved a room at a nearby restaurant for the family to gather for a meal.

"Go on ahead," Karl said to the others. "I'll join you. I want to stay here for a little while."

Beneath a cluster of spruce and linden trees, Karl sat on a little concrete bench and stared at the mound of soil sheltering Marlo's remains in the earth below. He studied thoughtfully the collection of potted plants and flowers that had been given to decorate Marlo's grave with splendid color—nature's celebration of her life.

Just then, a gust of wind broke loose one of the few remaining dainty heart-shaped leaves from a bough of a linden tree, the blossoms of which had long since disappeared in the summer's heat. Karl looked up to see that little heart flutter and come to rest on Marlo's grave. And he knew that, in many springs to come, linden blossoms would also blanket Marlo's hallowed ground. *How utterly appropriate, how unspeakably divine*, he thought.

Under the linden tree
Where blossoms fall gently down and covered me.

—Gustav Mahler

Made in the USA
Lexington, KY
14 April 2012